DRAGON'S
Breath

E. D. BAKER

SCHOLASTIC INC.
New York Toronto London Auckland Sydney
Mexico City New Delhi Hong Kong Buenos Aires

ISBN 0-439-67952-4

12 11 10 9 8 7 6 5 4 3 2 1   5 6 7 8 9 10/0

Printed in the U.S.A.   40

First Scholastic paperback printing, March 2005

Type set in twelve-point Garamond

This book is dedicated to Ellie, Kimmy, Nate and Emiko.
I would also like to thank Victoria Wells Arms
for asking the right questions.

One

When I was a little girl, I dreamed about being a witch like my aunt Grassina. I imagined that the next time a page stuck out his tongue at me, I'd wiggle my fingers and turn him into a salamander. If my nurse nagged me about the dirt on my clothes, I'd say a magic word and her voice would become a sparrow's chirp. If my mother scolded me for being clumsy and sent me to my chamber, I'd wave my hand, banishing her to some far-off cave guarded by trolls. I never did these things, of course, but I comforted myself with the thought that someday everyone who had been mean to me would be sorry. Someday I would be a witch and no one would dare tell me that I wasn't as smart or pretty or graceful as a princess ought to be.

Lately, I had decided that those dreams were a waste of time. Although my grandmother and aunt were both witches, my mother hated magic and let everyone know it. According to her, no self-respecting princess would ever be interested in magic, not if she really wanted to make something of herself. She threatened to send me to a convent if she ever saw me try it. "They'll know how to keep you too busy for such nonsense," she told me more than once.

If it hadn't been for my aunt Grassina, I might have given up my dream entirely, but she said I had a talent that shouldn't be ignored. I resolved not to tell my mother I planned to study magic, and my attempts remained a secret between my aunt and me.

In a way, I owed all the excitement in my life to my mother. Because she never seemed to want me around, I'd often wandered off to the swamp or to my aunt's tower chamber. Then, when my mother had tried to get me to marry a prince I couldn't stand, I hid in the swamp, unwilling to meet with him. There I met Eadric, a prince who'd been turned into a frog. I'd ended up kissing Eadric, and that kiss had turned *me* into a frog as well.

The morning after I returned home as a human, I was eager to work on my magic, if only to gain more control over my suddenly crazy life. I had never learned how to cook, so I thought I'd use a spell to make breakfast for Grassina and my no-longer-a-frog-friend Prince Eadric. I chose a recipe from one of Grassina's books, *Wolanda's Big Book of Recipes, Potions and Cooking Spells for the Inexperienced Witch*—"time-tested, witch-approved." It was a simple spell, one that even I should have been able to handle.

After fetching some peacock eggs from the kitchen, I hurried up the tower stairs to my aunt's rooms. Since my aunt often cooked her own meals, she already had everything else I needed. According to the directions, all I had to do was assemble the ingredients and the cooking spell would do the rest.

Li'l Stinker, a bat who had become a friend in my days of being a frog, greeted me at the door. The room was quiet; my aunt was probably still sleeping.

I'd decided to use Grassina's magic pot. Made of iron and black with age, it heated itself until the food was cooked. I'd never known Grassina to burn anything when she used the pot, and I hoped the same would be true for me.

Glancing from the pot to the book and back again, I was careful to read the spell aloud exactly as it was written.

> A pinch of this, a dash of that
> A hint of lard, a dab of fat
> A broken egg, no, make it three
> One's not enough, as you can see.
>
> Drop them in a cooking pot.
> Add some spice, no, not a lot.
> Chop an onion, put it in.
> Stir it once, then stir again.

Heat the pot until it cooks,
Sniff, then see how good it looks.
Get the dishes, serve it all.
Don't let the portions be too small!

Cooking spells are fun to watch, but I enjoyed watching Li'l even more. She chortled when the eggs cracked themselves and plopped into the pot. I heard her gasp when the onions broke into small pieces, then spiraled into the mixture with the spices.

When I read *sniff*, the steam rising from the eggs wafted toward my nose, drifting past Li'l. "Smells good," she said, breathing deeply. "Now what do you do?"

"I'll taste them, just to be sure they're all right. Then we'll invite Grassina and Eadric to breakfast."

Although I'd used only three eggs, the magic recipe had doubled them, so there was more than enough for everyone. Wondering if it had doubled the spices as well, I nibbled a tiny morsel. It needed salt, so I glanced toward the shelves holding my aunt's supplies. A small salt cellar rested on a high shelf beside jars of dried herbs. Pleased by my success with the cooking spell, I pointed at it and said, "Salt cellar," expecting it to fly into my hands. Straightforward and simple—I didn't think anything could possibly go wrong.

Two

Whoosh! A damp breeze whisked me from the stool where I'd been sitting, twirled me until I was dizzy and plopped me down on a lumpy sack somewhere cold and dark. Dazed, I shook my head and looked around. It could have been worse. At least I knew where I was: my parents' dungeon. And the door was most certainly locked.

I'd visited the dungeon often, but always dressed warmly and carrying a torch. It wasn't safe to walk around the dungeon in the dark. Unseen hands moved barrels, holes appeared where none had been before and doors that were centuries old suddenly disappeared. Witches had lived in the castle for generations, and here, where the early witches had set up their workshops, the magic had permeated the walls and still floated about in currents and eddies that smelled like rotting vegetables.

My mother, who wasn't a witch, had ordered the

dungeon cleaned out and now used it just for storage. But the witches' ghosts remained to haunt the old dungeon, and not all of them were friendly. My mother didn't believe in ghosts and kept the salt in the room where I now found myself, a long, narrow room that had once been used as the torture chamber. Why had I wanted salt for the eggs?

The torture chamber had no windows; not even the faintest glimmer disturbed the inky dark. I thought about using magic to go back upstairs, but I didn't know any spells that would take me from one place to another. Though I wanted to practice my magic, I didn't think I was ready to try to come up with my own spells yet, especially since it was a simple spell that had brought me to the dungeon. To get out safely, I needed some sort of light. A tethered witches' light would have to do, even though it would be vulnerable to the old magic wafting through the dungeon.

One of the first spells my aunt had taught me was for creating such a light. I'd used it many times, but only when Grassina was around. I recited the spell, shaping my hands as if I was holding a ball.

> Create a glow to chase the dark.
> A light to help me see.
> Let neither wind nor rain nor snow
> Take it away from me.

The space between my hands began to glow a rosy shade of pink as a ball of gentle light took form. I released the ball, and it drifted above my head.

I'd started toward the door when a whisper of sound behind me made me turn to look. A swirling mist glowing a faint blue poured through a hole in the wall. As the mist filled the room, a young woman appeared only a few feet away, her long tresses lifting in a nonexistent breeze. She gazed at me through shadowed eyes, her lips moving, her hands reaching in a pleading sort of gesture. An aura as cold as a winter's night surrounded her, giving me goose bumps as she drew near. Her lips moved again, and I strained to hear her words.

"I'm sorry," I said, tilting my head so that I might hear her better. "Could you repeat that?"

The ghost sighed and dropped her arms to her sides. "Then listen carefully this time," she yelled. "I *hate* repeating myself. I said, 'Help, help, save me. The executioner is coming and I've done nothing wrong.'" She spoke in a matter-of-fact sort of way, as if reciting lines that she'd repeated too often.

"Too late!" said a voice by the far wall. "I'm already here!" A broad-chested ghost dressed all in black materialized before us. His eyes glowed crimson through holes in the hood covering his head. Silently, the executioner wielded an axe, its blade dark with blood. The young lady shrieked and started to run. I closed my eyes, and when

I opened them, her head lay on the floor, gazing up in silent reproach.

"That was pretty good," I said, "although it works better when you delay your entrance, Cranston. It's more effective when Margreth convinces me of her innocence first."

"Sorry," said the executioner. "We're both a bit off today. We've had so many visitors lately, stomping around in heavy boots and thrusting torches in dark corners."

"Why were they here?" I asked.

Cranston shrugged. "Looking for something, I suppose. We're much better with the torture scene. Would you like to see that one? It's more realistic."

"No, thanks," I said, never having cared for the gruesome historic reenactments that some of the ghosts enjoyed. "I have too much to do this morning."

The ghosts disappeared, leaving me alone once again. I was stepping into the next room when my witches' light dimmed so much that I could hardly see. Something scrabbled against the stone floor like scores of metal-hard claws. I took another step, hoping to take the light out of the drifting pool of magic that had muted its glow.

A large shape loomed out of the dark, its glowing red eyes unblinking. If I hadn't encountered the creature before, I would have been terrified, but Grassina had shown me how to deal with it on one of our early visits. It was a shadow monster left behind by one of my ancestors and could be deadly to anyone who didn't know its weakness. I took one more step into the room, and the creature charged. It was almost upon me when I danced aside, rapping it between the eyes with my clenched fist. As the eyes were its only vulnerable spot, the shadow beast whined and fled into the old torture chamber.

I took another tentative step, not caring to fall into a bottomless pit or tread on a magic serpent created by an old spell. My witches' light grew brighter, lighting the darkened niches. I was halfway across the floor when a pale glow played around the edge of a door, outlining it in an eerie blue light. The light pulsed and wavered, seeming to seep through the door itself. It grew stronger the closer it came, finally taking on the shape of a man, taller than most, with shoulder-length white hair and finely chiseled features. Although the image remained translucent, I recognized him right away.

"Grandfather, you're back! I thought you were still away on ghostly business." I smiled up at the holes where his eyes should have been.

Clammy fingers touched my hand; the scent of old leather grew strong. "My darling Emma!" he answered, a chilly puff of air caressing my cheek. "I'm sorry I was away for so long. The meeting of the Council of Ghosts seems to last longer every year. I hear that you were away as well. Grassina told me something about a frog and a prince. You remind me of your grandmother. She was always doing the unexpected, too. Still is, from what I hear. You even look like her in a way."

"What?" I was horrified at the thought of resembling my grandmother in even the smallest detail. Although I had my father's large nose, I'd been told that with my taller-than-average height, auburn hair and green eyes I looked like my aunt Grassina. This was the first time anyone had ever compared me to my grandmother. Her long hooked nose, pointed chin, beady eyes, warts and straggly white hair were enough to frighten me, so I couldn't imagine that *anyone* would want to look like her. At least no one had ever accused me of acting like my grandmother.

"Olivene wasn't always like she is now. She was quite lovely when I married her, and was the sweetest and gentlest woman. It wasn't until your mother and your aunt Grassina were nearly grown that your grandmother changed."

"You're talking about the family curse, aren't you?"

"So you've heard about how the first Green Witch, Hazel, insulted a fairy?"

I had. It was Hazel's sixteenth birthday, and she didn't have enough everlasting bouquets to give one to the fairy. The fairy got angry and cursed Hazel: if she ever touched a flower, she'd end up nasty, like my grandmother was now. Aunt Grassina told me that the curse was still strong and that any female in our family who touched a flower after she turned sixteen would become a nasty hag.

"Oh, yes," I said.

"And you believe it?"

"Yes, of course. Why wouldn't I?" I asked.

"Because your grandmother didn't, at least not until it happened. Her mother had avoided flowers her entire life, but Olivene thought her mother was crazy, so she didn't believe her stories about the curse. After the curse changed her, your grandmother didn't care enough to do anything about it except send me to the dungeons."

"Is that how you ended up down here?"

A ghostly sigh brushed my ear. "Before the change, Olivene complained that I never took her to tournaments or balls at neighboring kingdoms anymore. I didn't know she wanted to go! I thought she was happy raising our girls and running the castle. She was always so busy with her magic. When your grandmother said that if I loved her I'd be more attentive and bring her little gifts, I tried to please her."

"You mean you're the one who gave her the flowers that turned her into—"

"Yes, I was the one. I had never heard of the curse, but ignorance is no excuse. After I gave her the flowers and she changed, she used her magic to send me to the

11

dungeon for a few days. I could have left anytime after that, but I liked the peace and quiet."

I could understand why he'd want to stay in the dungeon. I'd heard from my mother and my aunt how they had fought when they were young, and if my grandmother had been as nasty as she was now, the dungeon would have been the nicest place in the castle.

"I haven't seen your grandmother for years, but the funny thing is, I miss her. I saw your mother the other day, though. She stopped by to see if you were here. Chartreuse doesn't come down very often, I'm sorry to say. Why was she looking for you in the dungeon?"

"Maybe because she couldn't find me anywhere else. I kissed a frog named Eadric in the swamp. Then I became a frog, too. Until yesterday, that is. That's when I kissed him again with my charm reversal bracelet on and we both turned back into humans. Eadric is a prince and he wants to marry me, but I told him we had to wait and see."

"Do you love him? Your mother says that love isn't essential in a marriage, but it really is, you know. When we were young, I loved your grandmother so much."

"I guess I love him in a way," I said. I just didn't know if I loved him enough, not after seeing how much Grassina loved her betrothed, Haywood. He'd been missing for years; my grandmother had turned him into an otter. "But I'm not ready for marriage yet. I want to study magic first. Last night Aunt Grassina told me that if I work at it hard enough, I might be the Green Witch someday!"

"Just like her mother was before her."

"Grandmother was the Green Witch?"

"Before the curse took hold she was the nicest as well as the most powerful witch around. Those are both requirements for being the Green Witch." Grandfather floated beside me when I started toward the door. "Now, how did you get down here?" he asked.

"We're going to the Old Witches' Retirement Community this morning to see Grandmother and ask her to turn Haywood back into a human. She wants more grandchildren and my parents aren't about to have any more, so I think she'll do it. But I wanted to make a special breakfast first."

"Are you sure it's wise to ask your grandmother for help? She's a stubborn woman. You're going to have a difficult time changing her mind about Haywood."

"Even she has to see how much Grassina and Haywood love each other."

We were passing through a long corridor, and I could see the stairway leading out of the dungeon at the far end.

"OooOooOooO!" wailed a voice. "I smell a maiden with hair of flame—"

"Go on with you! You can't smell the color of her

hair!" said an older and less refined voice.

"I was being poetic!" said the first voice. "You should have let me finish!"

"Oh, go ahead, then. What else were you going to say?"

"I forget now! And it's a real shame because it was going to be beautiful!" The voice grew fainter.

At the approach of the ghosts, the temperature of the room had dropped even further. "I don't think I've met those ghosts before," I began. "They seem … ah … ah … ah-choo!" I knew right away that the sneeze wasn't an ordinary one. The tickling that had started in my nose filled my head, then rushed down my neck and into my entire body. I felt myself flash hot, then cold. My skin was suddenly sensitive to the air currents wafting through the dungeon, and I could clearly hear the sound of rats scurrying behind closed doors.

"Good gracious, child," said my grandfather. "What happened to you?"

"I don't know," I said, reaching for my tickling nose, but to my surprise, my nose wasn't there. "I think I …" I patted my face, then ran my hands over the top of my head, feeling the smooth, moist, hairless skin. "I can't believe this! I've turned back into a frog! What's wrong with me, Grandfather? Can't I do anything right? I … I … ah-choo!" I sneezed explosively, and suddenly I was back to my normal self.

"Are you all right, Emma?"

I patted my hair into place, glad that I had hair again. "Fine, I guess. But why did I change when I sneezed?"

"I can't help you there. I don't understand magic very well."

We had reached the end of the corridor and started to climb the stairs when I felt the tickling again. Not wanting to turn into a frog, I pinched my nose. When the urge to sneeze faded, I took my hand from my face and said, "I'd better go before … ah-choo!" I'd let go only briefly, but it had been enough. I was a frog once more.

"Perhaps if you sneeze again," said Grandfather, "you might turn yourself back."

It wasn't hard to do. I took a deep breath and felt the tickling sensation in my nose. The sneeze was coming, and it was going to be a big one! "*Ah-choo!*" I shot back up to my normal size and shape, but the tickling wasn't over. "*Ah-choo!*" My stomach lurched as I turned back into a frog. Too many changes too fast were more than it could take. "*Ah-choo!*" The instant I turned into a human again, I clapped my hand to my face and squeezed my nose so hard it hurt.

"Here!" said my grandfather, reaching through the door to unlock it. "Go before you change again! I love you no matter what shape you're in, but I'd much rather have a human granddaughter than one who's a frog!"

15

Three

As I hurried up the winding staircase to Grassina's turret, I tried to think of a way I could use magic to stop my froggy transformations. I was stepping onto the landing when I noticed that the door to my aunt's room was open. Inside, I saw Grassina and Haywood sitting on the window seat. It was obvious that their love was as strong as ever. For the first time I could remember, my aunt's eyes were as happy as her smile.

Grassina turned to look at me when I stepped into the room. "Wherever you went," she said, "it must have been awfully important to take you away before breakfast. It smells delicious. Thank you for making it."

"It needs salt," I said. "And I tried to use magic to get it. I pointed at the salt, said 'salt cellar,' and ended up in the dungeon."

Haywood winked at me and smiled. "These things happen," he said. "You just need to be more specific." Before turning into an otter, he had been a wizard in training and probably knew more about magic than I did.

"You're so wise, precious one," Grassina told the otter, stroking his ears.

"I saw Grandfather," I said before they could forget that I was there. "We had a nice visit, and he helped me find the way out. He said that Mother came down to look for me while I was away."

"Mm-hmm," murmured Grassina, leaning down to kiss Haywood's head.

Haywood turned to me. "Your mother must have been worried about you when you disappeared."

The door banged against the wall behind me, and Eadric rushed into the room. "There you are, Emma!" he said. "I've been looking for you everywhere. You wouldn't believe what happened while I was getting dressed. I was putting on my shoes when suddenly I turned back into a frog! It was so fast, too, not at all like the last time. I couldn't believe it at first, but it lasted only a little while, then suddenly I was back to being me. And then it happened again. What's going on? Yesterday when we turned back, I thought that everything would be all right."

"It wasn't only you, Eadric. I changed, too—every time I sneezed."

"Ah!" said Haywood. "You sneezed. That explains it!"

"I was afraid something like that might happen," Grassina said. "I was hoping you'd have more control of your magic before it did."

Eadric frowned. "I'm glad you understand. Now how about telling us?"

"It's simple, really," said my aunt. "Emma's magic is strong, and she has to learn how to control it. Until she does, whenever she stresses her body, that stress is going to snap her back to whatever form she was in last. That means that when she sneezed, which is an intense physical reaction, she became a frog. And remember that your spell was linked, so you both had to turn back into humans or you both had to remain frogs."

I couldn't believe my ears. I already had enough problems with my magic, and now this! "Why haven't I heard about this before?"

Haywood explained that it didn't happen often. Changing to another shape was generally discouraged among witches until they could exercise greater control, but in my case it wasn't a matter of choice.

"This could happen again?" I asked.

Grassina nodded. "I'm afraid so. You'll need to work on your magic as much as possible. It's controlling you now, and that's not a good way to live. I know you wanted to go with us to see your grandmother, but perhaps you should stay here."

I didn't like that idea at all. Sitting around the castle

worrying that I might turn back into a frog was the last thing I wanted to do. "I'd still like to go with you," I said. "I haven't visited Grandmother for a while, and Eadric wants to meet her before he returns to his parents' castle."

"What's that I smell?" Eadric asked. "Did someone make breakfast?"

"I did," I said. "Why don't you—"

Eadric hadn't waited to be asked. Grabbing a plate of eggs, he carried it to a bench by the wall. After popping a bite in his mouth, he said, "These eggs are delicious, but they could have used a little salt."

I rolled my eyes.

"I've met Emma's other relatives, and I've heard so much about her grandmother," Eadric said. "I'd like to meet her, too. Emma, you should have seen it!" he continued, turning to me. "Grassina sent a message to my parents saying that I'm all right. They can stop worrying now, and I can stay a while longer. I have to wait a few days for Bright Country, anyway. He still hasn't recovered from being turned back into a horse."

Haywood twitched his whiskers. "Do you know what you're getting into? Emma's grandmother has a nasty way with suitors."

"I'll tell her that we're friends," Eadric said. "She can't object to that. Hey!" he shouted, jumping to his feet. "Something pinched me!" Setting the plate on the bench, he rubbed his backside with one hand and thrust the other into the space between the bench and the wall, pulling out something small and golden brown. "Here's the culprit!" he said, waving it in the air.

"It looks like one of my crab-apple dumplings," I said. I had had enough experience with the nasty little things to recognize them even from across the room. Their flaky pastry had turned out well, but the claws they'd grown after my magic went awry could deliver a painful pinch. "I wouldn't eat it now. It's probably stale."

Freshness didn't matter to Eadric. After inspecting the golden brown crust and the squirmy, kicking legs, Eadric shoved the whole thing in his mouth and bit down. "Pretty good," he said through a mouthful of pastry. "Are there any more?"

"I hope not," I said, shaking my head. "But then, I thought we'd found them all weeks ago. Maybe the rest of us should have some eggs, too. Who knows when we'll get to eat again."

"I've already had my breakfast," said Haywood. "Fish, fresh from the pond. Best way I know to start the day."

It took less time to eat the eggs than it had to cook them. When she was finished, Grassina set her plate aside, and began to scratch Haywood behind his ears. Snuggling closer, he tilted his head from one side to the other. "That feels great," he murmured. "That's the spot!"

I grimaced and bit my lip. My normally calm, controlled aunt had not been herself since she found Haywood.

Grassina smiled and looked up at me. "Emma, you and Eadric are welcome to come with us if you want to, but there's no telling what might happen when your grandmother is involved. I'm not even sure if we should attempt this. Your grandmother can be quite hateful and—"

"Of course we should!" I said. "I'll talk to Grandmother. I'm sure she'll do it."

Grassina sighed. "No, I'll talk to her myself. She is my mother, after all. And perhaps she *will* turn him back. Even if she refuses, what more can she do? She's already turned him into an otter."

"I see the rumors are right, Grassina," said a voice from the doorway, and we all turned our heads at once. I was surprised to see my mother standing there. It had been years since she'd last visited her sister's chambers. Mother's lips were tight with disapproval as her gaze swept over us. "You do have an otter in your room. Why would you bring a creature like that into the castle?"

"He isn't a creature, Mother. At least that's not all he is," I said. "That's Haywood, the man that Grandmother didn't want Grassina to marry. Grassina discovered him by the river when she was helping us. Isn't it exciting that they finally found each other?"

"So, sister, our mother turned him into an otter and not a frog, as you believed. When I heard that an otter was up here, I was afraid that Emeralda had changed into another horrid animal since I last spoke with her. How are you, Haywood?"

"Just fine, Chartreuse. And I see you're still your same sweet self."

My mother frowned at the otter, then glanced at the wall behind him. A tapestry hung there, just as it had for years. It showed the image of a woman, her long auburn hair streaming behind her. She stood on the parapet of a castle with her arms upraised, and in each hand she held a glowing ball of green light. On the ground far below, the remnants of an army were in full retreat.

"Ah," said my mother. "The tapestry of the Green Witch. I remember the day you got this, Grassina. When we were little girls, who would have thought that you would end up with the title?"

"I know you thought it would be you, Chartreuse," Grassina said before turning to me. "When we were young, we'd often play at being witches, and your mother always insisted on being the Green Witch. She was devastated when we learned that I had the talent for magic and she didn't. But then, magic chooses its own, doesn't it, Chartreuse?"

My mother's eyes were cold, but she didn't say a word.

Haywood shoved his head into the palm of Grassina's hand, and my aunt bent down to scratch his ears. Mother groaned. "I have a bad feeling about this," she said to me in a quiet voice. "After they got engaged, Grassina couldn't think about anything but Haywood, whether he was around or not. It didn't matter so much then, but that was before she was the Green Witch. It isn't an empty title, you know, Emeralda. On the same day that Hazel, the first Green Witch, was given that tapestry, she received the ring Grassina wears now."

I glanced at my aunt, but I already knew which ring my mother meant. Carved from a single pale green gem, it looked like a band of tiny, overlapping leaves. She'd worn the ring for as long as I'd known her.

"Every Green Witch since Hazel has worn it. Both the ring and the tapestry symbolize the power wielded by the Green Witch. It's her power that protects this kingdom. Without a Green Witch in Greater Greensward, the kingdom would be vulnerable to attack."

Eadric had crossed the room to join us. "Are you talking about trolls and werewolves? Trolls invade my father's kingdom a couple of times a year, and the werewolves attack every winter."

"Really? We've never had any problems like that," I said.

"Most kingdoms aren't as fortunate as ours," said my mother. "Flocks of harpies, marauding goblins or packs of werewolves are drawn to kingdoms without a powerful witch or wizard to protect them. Just knowing that the Green Witch is here is enough of a deterrent for some, although she's forced to demonstrate her power occasionally."

"I've never seen Grassina fight anyone," I said.

"She hasn't had to for many years now. Her reputation is well known."

I didn't understand. I'd lived with my aunt my whole life, but this was all new to me. "I always thought it was Father and his knights who kept invaders away."

"Your father is a good man and terribly brave, but that means little to an army of trolls or a flock of harpies."

"Why didn't anyone ever tell me about this?"

"Because you never needed to know about it before," said my mother.

I heard a thud and turned in time to see Haywood scurry across a small table and peer into a bowl of water. A miniature castle rested in the bowl, but otherwise the water appeared to be empty. Licking his lips, Haywood stuck his muzzle in the water, then sat back on his haunches, making an awful face. "Ugh!" he said. "It's salty!"

"Oh, no, my heart's delight," exclaimed Grassina.

"You mustn't drink that!"

Mother crinkled her lip in disgust. " 'Heart's delight' is what she called him when they were young," she whispered. "We may have a problem if she's as besotted with Haywood as she used to be. She couldn't focus on anything that didn't concern him, and the rest of her life suffered from it. Our kingdom is in jeopardy if she's weak, no matter what the reason. Even now, trouble isn't far away. Your father should arrive home in a few hours, but he sent a courier on ahead. His men had discovered two spies at a local tavern. They escaped during the interrogation."

Eadric frowned. "Spies in Greater Greensward?"

Mother nodded. "We have to help Grassina come to her senses. She has to forget about Haywood and take care of her responsibilities here."

"No matter what form he's in, I don't think she'd ever forget about Haywood," I said. "But he may not be an otter for much longer. We're going to visit Grandmother today to ask her to turn him into a man."

"Grassina wants to ask her for help? Maybe my sister really is unbalanced."

"It was my idea," I said. "Grandmother turned him into an otter in the first place, so she's the one who has to turn him back."

Mother made a face as if she smelled something awful. "I've never known you to be so meddlesome before. Someone must have been a bad influence on you." She turned her glare on Eadric. "Whoever thought of it, the suggestion is ill-considered. My mother has never helped anyone except herself."

"If you can think of a better idea—" I began.

"Get rid of the otter. Haywood has complicated Grassina's life long enough."

"But she loves Haywood! She'd be miserable without him."

"Then get your grandmother to turn him back, but do it quickly." My mother shook her head when she glanced at Grassina and Haywood. "I have to prepare for your father's return. I must let him know what's happened here."

I walked with Mother to the door, hoping to hurry her out. "When I sent a message to your father telling him that you were home, I didn't mention your refusal to marry Prince Jorge," she said, pausing at the threshold. "I don't know how I'll break the news to him."

"I could tell him myself."

"Perhaps it isn't necessary. I've been considering the problem, and it's obvious to me that you haven't thought this through. If we keep your little frog-kissing adventure to ourselves, you can still marry Jorge." Mother's voice dropped to a whisper as she glanced at Eadric, who was eating again on the other side of the room. "No one need know that you've been a frog or disgraced yourself

26

with that young man."

"What are you talking about, Mother?" I asked, trying to keep my voice down as well. "Prince Eadric is a gentleman! We didn't do anything wrong."

"They're all gentlemen, until they have you alone."

"We were frogs!" I said. "We were trying to turn back into humans. What could—"

"It doesn't matter what you actually did. You were alone with a young man who wasn't related to you. That's all people need to hear. You know, of course, that's the worst thing that could have happened. Without beauty or grace, all you really had was your good reputation, and if your story gets out, you will no longer have that. But all may not be lost yet. If I hurry the wedding plans and you don't say a word to Jorge—"

"I'm not going to lie to him, Mother." I was sure that Jorge would hear about it eventually. Everyone in our castle probably already knew what had happened. It was nearly impossible to keep a secret with so many ears around.

My mother pursed her lips. "Then tell your tale as often as you'd like, but you've made a grave mistake. I don't know what your father and I will do with you now. I doubt that even a convent will take you."

"I shouldn't have bothered to come back at all!" I said.

"Perhaps you shouldn't have," Mother answered.

As soon as my mother was gone, Haywood spoke up. "Don't let your mother upset you, Emma, although if you want, I could take care of her for you. I was only a beginning wizard when Olivene transformed me, and not a very good one at that, but I remember some basic spells. It would be easy to turn Chartreuse into a magpie or squirrel. They all like to hear themselves chatter."

I laughed and shook my head. "Your offer is tempting, but I'd better not accept."

"If we're going to talk to *my* mother, we should leave soon," said Grassina. "Emma, why don't you and Eadric get the carpet from the storage room? The day is too beautiful to spend cooped up in a carriage, and Haywood would have difficulty staying on a horse. Ask Li'l where you can find the carpet."

It was dark inside the storage room, the only light coming through a window as narrow as an arrow slit. Eadric followed me through the door, stopping just inside when he saw the clutter. Something rustled in the rafters overhead, and I looked up. Li'l was hanging by her feet amid dangling bunches of herbs.

"Li'l!" I said. "It's me, Emma!"

"It's about time," the little bat squeaked. "Where did you go? One minute you were making breakfast, the next you were gone—poof!"

"I had a problem with my magic. I went to the dungeon by mistake."

"Those things happen," said Li'l, "especially when you're new at it."

"Do you know where my aunt put the carpet?" I peered into the darkened corners, where I could only make out vague shapes.

"Sure do! I know where everything is. Your aunt's put me in charge of inventory. The carpet's over there, behind that old mirror. Move the mirror aside … watch out, it tilts … that's it! There's the carpet."

The carpet was rolled up into a long tube, set on end so that it leaned against the wall. Eadric took one end and I took the other. It was heavy and awkward, but we'd soon wrestled it through the door and back into Grassina's sun-filled room.

Although the carpet was grimy on the outside, the colors were brilliant when we finally spread it in front of the window. Threads of scarlet, gold, navy blue, dark green and cream shone in the sunlight in a repeating pattern of flowers and abstract designs. A wide rug, it would hold the four of us easily.

Eadric stepped back to look. "It's very nice, but what does it have to do with going to your grandmother's?"

"This isn't an ordinary rug, Eadric. It's a magic carpet," said Grassina. "It will carry us wherever we want to go. It's a very comfortable way to travel as long as the weather is good."

Eadric turned to me. "Have you ever ridden on a magic carpet?"

"Never," I said, "but it looks like fun!"

"I'm not sure I want to trust anything involving magic yet," he said.

"You just ate a magic breakfast," I said.

"Here, Emma," said my aunt, holding out her hand. "Put these in your pouch. You never know when you might need them."

I did as she directed, tucking away an odd assortment of objects: a length of string, a small square of cloth and a candle stub. When everyone was ready, Eadric and I took our places on the magic carpet behind Grassina and Haywood. With a few softly spoken words, Grassina made the rug rise into the air. It moved in fits and starts, as if it wasn't quite sure what to do.

"I haven't used it for a while," my aunt said over her shoulder. "The ride should improve once the rug gets a good airing. Just stay seated and hold on."

"What about the window?" asked Eadric, his eyes enormous as the rug jerked toward the narrow opening. We were only inches away when the sides of the window stretched like a smiling mouth, allowing us to slip through easily. Once we were through, the window snapped back into place with a loud twang.

Grassina chuckled. "Don't worry, Eadric. This isn't the first time I've done this."

Four

The carpet dipped and swayed as it flew above the moat, until I was sure we were about to fall in. I grabbed hold of Eadric's arm, wishing I could hold something more stable, since he was shaking even more than the carpet. Rounding the last of the towers, the carpet leveled out and shot over the training fields where my father and his knights often practiced with swords and lances. In only a few minutes we had passed over the swamp that Eadric and I had spent days crossing. Beyond the river, we flew over the tops of trees, some so tall that I could nearly reach out and touch them.

The Old Witches' Retirement Community was located deep in the woods, accessible only by enchanted paths or by air. The paths led directly to the individual cottages and were the surest although slowest way of getting there. From the air, the community was so well hidden it would be easy to miss.

I tried to observe everything at once, turning my

head back and forth like a confused weather vane. Eadric was just as excited as I was, and together we made the rug jiggle and bounce as we looked around.

A pink fog drifted over the forest, its wispy tendrils reaching into the trees. The faint odor of boiled cabbage reached us, and I wondered who was cooking it. We were over the fog when I noticed the Purple Mountains in the distance. When I looked again, they seemed to be much closer. A hawk flew by, drawing my attention with it. The next time I looked toward the mountains, they appeared to have moved farther away again.

"Are the mountains moving?" I asked my aunt as the rug dropped closer to the woods.

"Not at all, although it looks that way, doesn't it? It's just the effect of the magic miasma, that pink fog that passes over the woods now and then. It's pretty, but it makes the community harder to find. Wait, I think I see it!"

The cottages of the Old Witches' Retirement Community were scattered around a small clearing. A fire pit occupied the center, an added bonus for those witches who liked to cook outside. Wooden tables and benches surrounded the fire pit, seating for the witches and their guests. The clearing was the first thing we spotted from the air. As we drew closer, I began to see the cottages hidden among the trees.

There were four basic styles of cottages, but each

witch had decorated hers in her own way, so no two were exactly alike. Some of them were gingerbread houses like my grandmother's, some walked about on chicken legs and some had thatched roofs and were surrounded by bushes bearing red and white roses; others were made of stone and covered with ivy.

The community itself grew and shrank as witches came and went, the cottages lasting only as long as they were needed. Some, like the gingerbread houses, disintegrated over time if not maintained. The cottages with chicken legs walked away when their owners died.

The rug was skimming just above the tops of the trees when I spotted Grandmother's cottage. Made of gingerbread, it had been repaired so many times that it didn't look at all the way it had when it was new. Visitors had eaten most of the icing trim, and my grandmother had replaced it with spun sugar. The gumdrops decorating the shutters had gotten hard, so she'd set clear fruit-flavored lozenges in their place. She'd also had to replace the gingerbread doors and many of the more accessible sections of the walls. The newer pieces of gingerbread were darker in color than the older ones, giving it a patchwork kind of look.

Grassina landed the rug in the cottage's front yard, and I expected Grandmother to tear out of the house, waving her broom at us and screeching her usual greeting. When she didn't even peep out from behind her cotton-candy curtains, I became concerned. Scrambling to my feet, I hurried to her front door. The latch, made of licorice and bearing the teeth marks of some long-ago visitor, was so sticky that I didn't want to touch it, but I didn't have much choice.

Lifting the latch, I pushed the door open and peeked inside. "Grandmother! Are you there? It's me, Emma! Grassina's here, too!"

Aside from the normal creaking of a candy house, the cottage was silent. *That's strange,* I thought, stepping into the tiny entranceway. The cottage was small, so it didn't take me long to search it, but there was no sign of Grandmother in the kitchen, the parlor or either of the two guest bedrooms. I didn't really expect to find her in her bedroom at that time of day, but I glanced inside anyway. I was closing the door when I noticed a lump under her bedcovers. Tiptoeing into the room, I reached for the covers and yanked them back, but it was only her cat, Herald, taking a nap. An old orange tabby turning white around the mouth and eyes, Herald was the only animal I'd ever known my grandmother to like, and was one of the most disagreeable cats I'd ever met.

Blinking sleepy eyes at the sunlight flooding the room, Herald put his ears back and growled when he saw me. I was used to his temper, however, and knew enough to keep well away from his claws.

"I don't suppose you know where my grandmother

is," I said, not really expecting an answer.

The cat sneered, then sat up to lick the base of his tail. I turned to leave and was halfway out the door when Herald spoke up. "Even if I knew, I wouldn't tell you. You've never treated me the way I deserve to be treated. No self-respecting witch's cat wants to be cuddled and called baby names!"

"I'm sorry I offended you, but I know a lot of cats who like to be petted," I said.

Herald stretched out a leg and bent down to lick his thigh. "Well, I'm not one of them!" He glanced up at me and crinkled his nose in a half snarl. "At least you're working on your magic, although you're long overdue."

"How do you know what I'm doing?"

"You're talking to me, aren't you? Your grandmother will be pleased. She's been very disappointed in you lately. As for where you can find her, she disappeared a few nights ago. It's a good thing she put in that cat door or I might have gotten hungry by now."

I left the cat bathing himself and went outside to find Grassina. Hearing sounds in the backyard, I headed around the side of the cottage, passing Grandmother's rock candy sundial on the way. It was almost noon, Grandmother's normal lunchtime. She should have been there, setting the table for her midday meal.

When I found my aunt, she was kneeling beside the oversized oven that Grandmother used for baking large sheets of gingerbread. "What are you doing?" I asked.

"Checking to make sure she isn't in here," said Grassina. "She once had a neighbor who had some children visit for a few days. One of them shoved her in her own oven and slammed the door shut. All that was left of her were some charred bones."

"That's terrible! What happened to the children?"

"Not a thing. They said that she was going to eat them, and claimed it was self-defense."

I shuddered. "Was there anything in Grandmother's oven that shouldn't be there?"

Grassina shook her head.

Munching a piece of gingerbread he'd taken from someone's wall, Eadric came out of the forest with Haywood loping by his side.

"I think Grandmother's been gone for a few days," I said.

When Grassina raised a questioning eyebrow, I told her of my encounter with Herald the cat.

"I'm not surprised that you can't find her," said Eadric. "Haywood and I took a quick look around, but we didn't see a single witch."

"That's right," said Haywood. "I think this whole place is abandoned."

"Maybe we should check the other cottages," I said.

Grassina nodded. "We probably should. Just don't open any doors. These old witches don't take kindly to nosy people. Now be careful."

I joined Eadric outside the gate while Haywood accompanied Grassina. None of the cottages we found appeared to be occupied.

Once we had finished, Eadric and I headed for the clearing in the center of the community. We had reached the first of the tables encircling the fire pit when Eadric stopped and bent down to pick up something. "What's this for?" he asked, showing me a simple cloth bag.

I turned it over in my hands. "I don't know. Maybe we should show it to Grassina." I jumped when Haywood leaped onto the table beside me, landing with a thud.

"What do you want to show her? Here, let me see." The otter sniffed it, then weighed it with his paws before setting it on the table. "Seems harmless enough. Queen of my heart, come see this!"

Grassina stepped up to the table and passed her hand over the bag as if she was feeling for something. "There's nothing magical about it. Let's see what it holds." When her nimble fingers had untied the knot, she poured some of its contents onto her palm. Pure white sand the color of fresh snow formed a sparkling mound.

"It's sand!" said Eadric, sounding disappointed. "Why would anyone put sand in a little bag like that?"

"That's a good question, Eadric," said my aunt.

"Something is very wrong here. All of the witches seem to have left at once, although there were no fires, no threat of any kind and no obvious reason why they should leave. These witches wouldn't just abandon their homes or their animals, not with all the magic they have tied up in them. Keep looking and see what else you can find."

Once again, Eadric and I went in one direction, while Grassina and Haywood went in the other, inspecting the tables and the area around them. The fire in the fire pit had gone out, another sign that something was wrong, since the witches always kept it lit. Ashes from the pit had blown across the clearing, drifting all the way to the inner circle of tables. I was holding my skirts out of the ashes, nudging a lump with the toe of my shoe, when I noticed a mouse under the table.

Seeing that the mouse was running toward a small hole in the ground, I darted ahead and covered the hole with my foot. "Excuse me," I said, crouching down so that I was closer to its level. The mouse skidded to a stop, sitting back on its haunches in surprise. "I see that you're in a hurry, so I won't keep you long. I was wondering if you could tell me where the witches have gone."

The mouse looked over its shoulder as if expecting to see someone else standing behind it. When it realized that there was no one there, it turned back to stare up at me. "You're talking to me? No big people ever talk to me!"

"It's true, I am talking to you, but then I happen to know that mice can be very nice. My name is Emeralda. My grandmother lives in the retirement community, and her name is Olivene. I can't seem to find her or any of the other witches who live here. I was wondering if you might know where they went."

"I have no idea where the witches went, but the other evening they had a big meeting with lots of people talking. Then they all got excited and flew off with parchments in their hands that looked like that one." The mouse pointed at the ground.

Reaching under the table, I felt something beneath the ash. It was a parchment, so coated with ash that the writing was barely discernable. When I picked it up and shook it, I realized my mistake instantly. My nose began to tickle. I tried to hold the sneeze in, but it was too strong. My eyes began to water, feeling as if they might pop out of my head if I didn't sneeze. I looked around, wanting to warn Eadric … and then … "*ah-choo!*"

I've never been able to keep my eyes open when I sneeze, so I didn't see Eadric change. When I opened them, I was chest deep in the powdery ash, holding the edge of the parchment in my long green fingers. The mouse took one look at me and disappeared into its hole.

"Emma!" Eadric wailed.

"I'm over here," I said, waving my other hand in the air.

"Don't just sit there!" he said, his voice growing louder as he hopped toward me. "Turn us back!"

"I'll try," I said. If the ash made me sneeze once, it ought to do it again. Leaning toward the dust, I took a deep breath, but instead of sneezing, I started to cough, a loud hacking cough that reached deep into my lungs.

Eadric emerged from the ash like a small, lumpy ghost. He looked so funny that I would have laughed if I hadn't still been coughing. "How about a spell?" he asked. "Grassina said you'd have to learn to control the frog transformations through your magic."

"My magic! But I don't know any spells to turn us back."

"Then make one up. It can't be too hard. Witches make up spells all the time."

"I suppose I could try," I said, but my mind was already whirling. *Should I make it rhyme? What if I turn us into something horrible? What if the witches return and throw me in a cauldron before I can explain who I am? What if—*

"Are you going to make up a spell or not?" asked Eadric. "This ash is drying me out. We're going to have to find some water if you don't change us back soon."

"All right, all right. Just give me a minute!" *Frog, clog, dog, bog* ... I tried to think of rhyming words that I could use. *Change, strange, range* ... Although I had a good idea of what a spell could do, I had no idea how it worked.

"If you're not going to try a spell, I'm heading for those trees," said Eadric. "It's too hot here, and my skin is starting to shrivel."

"Fine, fine," I said. "I'll try this one."

> I'm now a frog.
> I was a girl,
> Please turn me back
> And make—

"No, wait!" shouted Eadric. "Think about what you're saying! You're still a girl, just not a human girl. Try again ... something that doesn't involve gender. The last thing I want to do is turn into a girl."

"Okay," I said. "Then how about this?"

> Frog isn't what
> I want to be.
> Please turn me in-
> To my old me.

I could feel myself changing, although it wasn't at all like the other times. I grew bigger and taller, but I also felt weaker. I felt pains in my joints and my vision blurred. When I looked at my hands, they were human, but they were wrinkled and had brown spots on the back. I turned to look at Eadric and saw an old man with a pot-belly and straggly white hair sitting in the ash.

"Here they are!" shouted a familiar voice, and Haywood came sliding on his stomach through the dust. "I found the old witches ... but there's only two. And one looks like an old man."

"One *is* an old man," grumbled Eadric, his voice as creaky as rusty armor. "An old man who should be a young one. What's wrong with you, Emma? Can't you get anything right?"

"I told you I didn't have a spell ready, Eadric," I said, my own voice sounding shrill in my ears. "But you insist-ed that I—"

"Emma, Eadric, is that you?" Grassina stepped light-ly through the ash. "Good gracious! What happened?" she said, glancing from Eadric to me.

Eadric scowled. "We were frogs, so Emma tried to use her magic to make us human again."

"I said I wanted to be turned into my old me. I guess I shouldn't have said *old*."

"No," said Grassina, "but at least this is one spell that's easily reversed." Taking a burnt piece of wood from the fire pit, Grassina scribbled something on a scrap of parchment she dug from her pouch, then hand-ed it to me, saying, "Read this out loud, Emma."

I had to squint to read it, as my vision wasn't very

good, but she'd printed the letters large enough that it wasn't too hard.

> From old to young,
> Return us to
> Our rightful age,
> To each be true.

I sighed with relief when the aches and pains melted away. My scalp prickled when my hair turned from white to its normal auburn; my skin tingled as it grew firmer and the wrinkles disappeared. My eyesight improved as well, and everything that had been blurry came into focus. Although it didn't happen all at once, it was fast enough to be disorienting, and I had to grab Grassina's hand to keep my balance.

"Oh, my!" I said, closing my eyes until the world stopped spinning. "I'm glad that's over."

"Suddenly I feel sorry for the old witches," Eadric said. "Being old is terribly uncomfortable."

"How did it happen, Emma?" asked Grassina.

"Oh!" I said, glancing at the ground by my feet. "A mouse showed me a parchment. I picked it up and the dust made me sneeze. Here it is."

Careful to hold my breath, I retrieved the parchment from the ash and shook it clean. It was beautiful. Done in the style of the best illuminated manuscripts, a small picture depicted a dark and gloomy swamp where trees stood on stilted roots above a winding river. Toothy reptiles propelled themselves through the water with their long, ridged tails, while slender, beady-eyed snakes twined around branches. The text was handwritten in black ink with gold accents and looked very fancy.

Tired of retirement? Forget all your troubles and begin life anew in the Forgotten Swamp.

Eadric examined the creatures in the picture. "Look at the size of those things! Do you suppose they're real?"

"Maybe, but if they are, I wouldn't want to be a frog in that swamp!" I said.

Grassina, however, seemed even more impressed when I repeated what the mouse had told me. "Wonderful!" she said. "Now we have a good chance of finding the old witches."

Five

Grassina stuck two fingers in her mouth and whistled three distinct notes. She had scarcely finished when the magic carpet appeared over the tops of the trees. I tried to be careful stepping onto the carpet, but the ash I stirred up made my eyes water. Squeezing them shut, I wiped my eyelids with my handkerchief and held my nose so I wouldn't sneeze. When I could see again, I noticed that Grassina had taken her black dragon's scale out of the pouch on her belt.

"Is everyone ready?" she asked, settling her skirts around her.

Eadric took my hand and I glanced at his face. He was pale and his lips were pressed in a tight line. Realizing that he might be nervous about flying, I smiled at him in what I hoped was a reassuring manner and gave his hand a squeeze. "You don't have to go. We can drop you off at your parents' castle."

Eadric shook his head. "I'm going if you are. You

need me to keep you safe."

"I'll be fine—" I began, but from the set of his jaw, I knew he wasn't about to change his mind. "We're as ready as we'll ever be," I told Grassina.

Clutching the small bag of sand and the parchment in one hand, Grassina held the scale in the other and said,

> Witches who around here sat
> Suddenly decided that
> They had someplace new to go,
> As this picture seems to show.
>
> Use these things to help us find them.
> Let no one in secret bind them.
> Be it near or be it far,
> Show us where these witches are.

I peered over my aunt's shoulder to see the scale. A gift to Grassina from a dragon friend, the scale was an excellent direction finder, with sparks of light flashing red for hot when aimed in the right direction, and blue for cold when aimed the wrong way. My legs were beginning to cramp by the time the light flashed. It was blue at first, but my aunt tilted her head and the rug lifted a few inches off the ground, rotating slowly until the light changed to red.

Grassina muttered something under her breath and the rug rose into the air, its movement smoother than when we had left the castle. Rising above the treetops, the rug swayed in the air currents, settling down only after Grassina used a calming spell.

The lights sparking through the scale were faint, a good indication that we had far to travel. Before long, we were moving so fast that we had to squint against the wind. Although I tried to look at the scenery, I soon gave up and closed my eyes, clinging to Eadric's hand as the wind buffeted the carpet. I opened my eyes once and we had passed the Purple Mountains. I opened them again and we were flying over a vast plain where an army marched below us, so far away that they looked smaller than ants.

When daylight faded into night and the stars came out one by one, I closed my eyes and leaned against Eadric. I must have slept, for the next thing I knew it was daylight and we were flying over a body of water that seemed to go on forever. At one point, a group of enormous fishlike creatures passed below us, clearly visible despite the great distance that separated us. I wanted to share the sight with Eadric, but when I glanced at him, his face was pale, the skin around his mouth slightly green.

"Are you all right?" I asked.

Eadric moaned and shook his head, his lips pursed

shut as if speaking would take too much effort. I squeezed his hand. A moment later, he leaned toward the edge of the rug and emptied his stomach to the water below. I felt sorry for him when he finally sat up, pale and shaking, although I was grateful that the wind carried the smell away.

Most of our trip had been made in good weather, but as the hours passed, the sky grew cloudy and white-caps topped the waves. Eadric moaned more often now, and his hand felt cold and damp. *We need to set down soon,* I thought, and leaned forward to check the scale again. The lights were brighter, the red sparks flashing with such frenzy that I knew we were approaching our destination.

"Do you know where we are?" I asked, leaning close to my aunt's ear.

"I have a good idea. There's an island straight ahead. It's where we're headed if I'm not mistaken. Sit back and hold on tight. Our ride is about to get rough."

Despite the spell my aunt had used to keep us steady, the magic carpet jerked and shuddered as the wind increased. Now Grassina took us higher still. The clouds appeared dark and menacing, and I dreaded going through them. When we entered the first cloud, a chill enveloped us that made my breath catch in my throat. I shivered as the cold seeped into my bones. Eadric was only a vague shape beside me, though he was so close our hips touched.

The wind grew stronger, lashing us with rain. Looking up as lightning flashed, I saw the otter slipping toward the edge of the rug. "Haywood!" Grassina screamed, and lunged for him, grabbing his furry paw as he was about to go over. The otter scrabbled with his hind paws, dragging himself back onto the rug until he was huddled by my aunt, her arm pressing him to her side.

My stomach lurched when the carpet dropped and then shot up again just as quickly. Clutching the carpet's edge on one side and Eadric's hand on the other, I was truly frightened for the first time since our journey began. My heart thudded as the rug bucked and swooped. Damp and shivering, I bit my lip, trying not to cry out when I felt the tickling begin. Alarmed, I pressed my nose against my shoulder, but it wasn't enough. The tickling became unbearable, and I squeezed Eadric's hand in warning.

Of course I sneezed. The transformation was almost instantaneous. No longer a gradual tingling, it felt more like a shock that started in my fingers and toes, then coursed through my body until it reached my head, making it feel fizzy and light. When I glanced down, I saw smooth green legs jutting out before me. Looking up, I saw Eadric's froggy mouth hanging open in dismay.

Unable to hold on to the rug with our small fingers,

we were helpless against the rushing wind. The next powerful gust blew us off the rug and we fell, tumbling through the air, our intertwined fingers all that kept us together.

I screamed, the sound carried away by the wind as we plummeted through the cloud, head over heels, twisting and turning until I wasn't sure which way was up. When I saw the terror on Eadric's face, I realized that I was the only one who could save us. With all the wind and rain, my aunt probably didn't even know that we had fallen.

The wind tried to tear us apart, but we held on, gripping each other's hand as hard as we could. Flipping over again, I found myself looking down at the water as it rushed up to meet us. My eyes were streaming from the wind, but even so, the waves looked far too close to me.

I forced myself to concentrate. There had to be something … I tried to remember all the spells I'd read, but none of them seemed appropriate. I had to come up with a spell of my own. What if some kind of creature could meet us partway and take us to the island? A bird, perhaps. I shouted the spell as I thought of it, although I doubt volume makes much difference when it comes to magic.

> Winged creature flying near,
> Save us from the death we fear.
> Catch us now before we land
> On the water or the sand!

I turned my head this way and that, hoping to spot a seabird braving the winds to rescue us. When nothing came, I closed my eyes and squeezed Eadric's hand, sorry that I'd gotten him into such a mess. Tumbling through the air, I expected to splat against the water at any moment, so I didn't know what to think when I hit something tough and leathery that gave beneath my body. I became even more confused when I opened my eyes. We had fallen onto a broad, black back, hurtling just above an enormous wave.

"Hang on!" shouted a voice, but there was nothing to hold on to except the rippling, leathery edge of the creature. Eadric and I grabbed hold just as the creature hit the water and plunged under the surface. I felt the pressure change when the wave roared over our heads.

What kind of bird is this? I wondered, peering through the churning water. We went deeper, gliding beneath the waves where the water was dark and murky. I studied the creature as best I could, but it didn't make any sense. It had neither feathers nor wings, yet it flapped like a bird. Its great, wedge-shaped body was smooth and black with a pair of curled horns, yet it had no head that I could see. There was no animal on dry land to compare it to, so I didn't know if we should be relieved at our rescue or terrified that this creature had found us.

"How are you doing?" the creature asked in a bubbly sort of voice. As I couldn't locate its face, I didn't know what part of the creature I should address.

"Who are you?" I asked, my own voice sounding strange underwater.

"They call me Manta. So, what are you two? I've never seen fish like you before, and you don't have fur like seals."

Eadric laughed. "We're not fish. We're frogs, or at least we are now."

"Frogs, huh?" Manta said. "Never heard of frogs before. You must be rare."

"As rare as enchanted royalty," Eadric said, puffing himself up.

"That's not rare. I wish I had a mouthful of plankton for every enchanted prince I've met. Speaking of plankton, do you mind if I have a snack?" Manta rose toward the surface while unfurling his horns, which I realized weren't really horns at all, but a way to funnel cloudy water into what had to be his mouth.

"You don't suppose he eats frogs, do you?" I whispered into Eadric's eardrum.

Eadric peered ahead to where the cloudy water was disappearing at an amazing speed. "I doubt it. From the looks of things, I think he prefers soup."

Another wave curled over our heads. I grabbed hold of the creature's smooth-skinned edge, gasping as he plunged into the heart of the wave. Flying beneath the violence of the surface, Manta's body rose and fell as his triangular wings propelled us through the water. His rhythmic movements were soothing and much more comfortable than the flying carpet. It would have been peaceful if it weren't for the muffled roar of the storm and the strange booms and wails that grew clearer as Manta dove.

"What's that sound?" I asked.

"Just the whales talking," Manta gurgled. "They say the storm is ending."

After a while, the voices of the whales died away, replaced by a series of high-pitched chirps and whistles. "Is that another whale?" I asked.

"That's a porpoise. Those guys are such comedians. They're always coming up with new jokes. Hey, have you heard this one? Why did the porpoise cross the ocean?"

"How would we know?" said Eadric. "We've never even met a porpoise!"

"You don't have to meet one. It's a joke! Come on, let's try it again. Why did the porpoise cross the ocean?"

"I don't know," I said. "Why?"

"To get to the other tide."

Eadric grunted and made a face.

"I'm sorry we don't understand your joke, Manta, but we're not familiar with the ocean. We've come a long way to find my grandmother," I said. "She's on an island near here and needs our help."

Manta dipped a wing and turned abruptly. "There's

only one island around this part of the sea. I'll have you there in three shakes of a mermaid's tail. Hold tight, I'm going up to look around."

Flapping his wings in long, powerful strokes, Manta sped to the surface, shooting straight into the air, and twisting before he fell. The sun had come out, and the clouds were disappearing on the horizon. Although the waves were still high, they were nothing like they'd been only a short time before.

An island stood off to our right. It was a beautiful place, with strange, frond-topped trees and a pure white shore. I caught a quick glimpse of huts and people in brightly colored clothes, but Manta flopped back into the water before I could see much more.

Circling the island, Manta brought us close to shore at a lonely spot well past the huts. I plopped into the shallows beside Eadric, who scrambled out of the water as quickly as he could. Holding on to Manta so that the waves wouldn't carry me away, I said, "Thank you for helping us. Most creatures wouldn't have bothered."

"It was my pleasure," he replied, his edges rippling. "I love meeting strange creatures, and you two are some of the strangest I've ever met!"

Six

adric had waited for me at the water's edge. He was frowning, and I knew he wasn't in a good mood. "Grassina was right when she said you should work on your spells. What were you thinking of with that last one? Winged creature? You could have called up anything from a gnat to a dragon!"

"I was trying to call a bird."

"Some bird!" he said.

"At least I tried! I didn't see you doing anything to save us."

"Huh!" said Eadric. He turned away and hopped stiffly up the beach. I followed only a few paces behind, tired, thirsty and with a terrible headache.

"We have to find fresh water," I said to Eadric's rigid back.

"That's where I'm going now," he grumbled. "I thought I saw sunlight reflecting off water behind these trees."

"I hope you're right," I muttered.

Although the rain had cooled the sand temporarily, it was already becoming hot beneath our feet. I tried to make long hops so that my feet didn't have to touch the scorching ground as often.

I was trying to keep up with Eadric when I bumped into a brown ball covered with coarse, thick hairs. The ball rolled aside, revealing a small green crab. I backed away when the crab clacked its claws in the air. A chorus of claws sprang up around me; I was surrounded by crabs even bigger and meaner than the first one.

"Eadric!" I shouted, hopping from one vacant patch of ground to another as more crabs threatened me with their claws.

"Over here, Emma!" Eadric had passed most of the crabs before they noticed us. I hopped again, but a crab scuttled forward unexpectedly and I landed on his back, flipping him over when I jumped again.

A dozen or so scurried to block my path. "This way!" Eadric shouted.

The crabs scuttled after him, leaving an opening. I knew I wouldn't stand a chance against the oversized claws of the larger crabs, so I hunched down, tensed my muscles and leaped as far as I could, flying over their heads. Although I made it past the crabs, I landed face first, getting a mouthful of sand.

We hopped away as fast as we could and didn't stop

until we landed in the freshwater pond Eadric had seen. While Eadric paddled across the pond, I rinsed the sand from my mouth, spitting until the grit no longer rasped my tongue.

The water was warmer than I was used to, and felt wonderful. Still, I couldn't wait to start looking for Grassina. Even if she'd landed safely, I was sure she'd be worried about me. But before we went anywhere, we needed to turn back into humans. There was no telling what other kinds of creatures we might meet on the island.

Not wanting to make myself prematurely old again, I was reluctant to try another spell, so I began to look around, wondering what I might use to make myself sneeze. I saw Eadric chasing insects at the water's edge and was about to call to him when I spotted the most beautiful crimson flowers. They didn't look real with their golden centers and long, curled petals, and I couldn't resist the urge to touch them.

I'd always been fascinated by flowers, perhaps because they were forbidden in my parents' castle. When I was younger, I'd been told that my mother and aunt were allergic to them, and I'd only recently learned the truth about the family curse. Since the curse didn't take effect until after one's sixteenth birthday and I had yet to turn fifteen, I was still immune.

I could smell the flowers' perfume even though I was

yards away. Climbing out of the water, I reached for a stem, pulling it down until I had the blossom cupped in my hands. The tingling began with my first sniff. I took another breath, deeper than the first.

"Eadric!" I shouted. "I'm going to … going to … *ah-choo!*"

The fizzy rush happened almost instantly. One moment I was a frog standing on tiptoe, sniffing a flower, the next I was a princess, crouched over a flower that I still cradled in my hands. I heard a shout and saw Eadric climbing from the pond, his clothes and hair streaming water. He wore the silliest grin, and I couldn't help but laugh. I guffawed, I chortled, I wheezed, just as I always do. Some unseen creature thrashed about in the foliage by the edge of the pond. A flock of shrill-voiced birds exploded from a nearby tree, scattering leaves and loose feathers. Eadric joined in, laughing so hard that he bent double, his arms wrapped around his stomach.

"Don't ever change your laugh, Emma," said a voice. "It's a wonderful way to find you." My aunt Grassina stepped into the sunlight surrounding the pond. Her hair hung down her back and was even more disheveled than usual. Bits of leaves peeped from the snarled curls, and wet sand smeared her clothes. Haywood scampered at her side, his drying fur ruffled and crusted with sand.

"Grassina!" I shouted. Scrambling to my feet, I ran to give my aunt a hug and to tell her the story of how we'd met Manta. "So what happened to you after we fell off?" I asked as we joined Eadric by the pond.

"It was a fight the whole way. I didn't notice you were missing until we had almost reached the island. When I saw that you were gone, I had the rug circle back. It never occurred to me that you might have turned into frogs again. No wonder we couldn't find you!"

"What did you do then?" I asked.

"We came to the island to wait out the storm," said Haywood, "but the wind had gotten stronger and we had a rough landing."

"Did you see the swamp from the sky? Did you see Grandmother or any of the other witches?"

Grassina shook her head. "We didn't see much of anything, but I don't think there's a swamp. The island isn't very big."

"The picture on the parchment—" Eadric began.

"Was a trick to get the witches here, if I'm not mistaken," said my aunt. "Knowing that group, a snake-infested swamp would be more of an attraction than a tropical beach."

"Do you suppose the witches might be on the beach? Eadric and I saw people and huts."

"Then that's where we should start looking. Come along, sugarplum," Grassina said, ruffling Haywood's fur. "Let's go see if we can find my mother."

I wasn't happy about walking beneath the trees since

I didn't want to encounter the crabs again, but there wasn't any way to avoid it. I didn't have to worry, however. The moment Haywood saw the crabs, he licked his lips and galumphed across the sand in pursuit of a large fat one, sending the rest into hiding. While Grassina waited for him to return, Eadric and I kept walking.

We were alone among the trees when Eadric said, "So how about a kiss? I haven't had one yet today." He took a step closer, backing me against one of the frond-topped trees, and leaned toward me with his hand braced against the trunk.

"A kiss? With all the things we have to do, is that all you can think about?"

Eadric grinned. "Sometimes. Other times I think about horses or improving my swordplay or what I'm going to have for dinner, but none of those things seem important when we're alone on this beautiful island."

"You mean I'm more important than horses right now?"

"And dinner. My stomach hasn't settled down yet, so I'm still not hungry. Do I get that kiss?"

I rolled my eyes. "After that romantic explanation it would be almost impossible to refuse, but I'll manage," I said, ducking under his arm.

"Hey!" said Eadric. "What's wrong? You kissed me the other day."

"You're right, I did. I must not have had anything

more important to think about then."

With Eadric trailing behind, I hurried between the last of the trees and stepped onto the beach. There were people there, scattered across the sand like brightly colored flowers. All elderly women, they were dressed in loose-fitting gowns made from vibrant fabrics. The sleeves were short, leaving the women's arms exposed. Although my mother would have been shocked, I thought it was practical for such a hot climate. I was already perspiring in my long-sleeved gown.

Small groups of women strolled along the water's edge, giggling when the waves wet their feet and legs. They'd stop now and then to pick up objects that the storm had washed ashore, exclaiming over their finds like children on a treasure hunt.

Other women were working on their own projects. The closest of these was an old woman in a yellow and orange gown kneeling beside a castle she was constructing out of sand. Since the castle was within the water's reach, she was constantly repairing walls and towers, scooping the sand with a large seashell.

"Hello!" she said, looking up as we drew near. "Come to see my castle? It's a beauty, isn't it? Watch what happens when the water fills the moat. See, it looks just like the real thing!" Water from one of the larger waves had run hissing up the sand, filling the moat and lapping at the castle walls. Clapping her hands, the old woman sat back on her heels and watched the wave retreat.

"You've done a beautiful job," said Grassina, coming through the copse of trees. "Did you build it all by yourself?"

"Of course. No one else can handle the sand so well. I'm the only one who can fashion a bridge or mold towers like these," she said, patting one tenderly.

"So you know everyone on the island?"

The old woman nodded. "There aren't that many of us. We all live right there," she said, pointing toward a nearby group of huts.

"I know that woman," Grassina muttered once we'd continued on our way. "But I'd swear she didn't recognize me. Her name is Hennah, and she isn't behaving like herself at all."

"She seemed nice," I said, glancing back over my shoulder.

"Yes, she does, which isn't like her. Normally, she hates people and goes out of her way to let them know it."

"All the witches from the retirement community must be here. We should have asked Hennah where we could find Grandmother."

"There's another witch," said Eadric, pointing farther down the beach. "Let's ask her."

An old woman with curling white hair so long that it brushed the sand was bent double, collecting seashells.

She looked up when our shadows crossed her path.

"Good day," said Grassina. "I was wondering if I might ask you a question. Do you know anyone named Olivene?"

The old woman straightened and brushed a strand of hair from her eyes. "I don't think so," she said in a husky sort of voice.

"Could you tell us your name?" I asked.

The old woman looked perplexed. "I can't seem to remember…."

"That's all right," I hurried to tell her. "Sorry to have troubled you."

The old woman held up her cupped hands, opening them to reveal an assortment of shells. "Would you like to see my seashells? I've found some lovely ones. Some of these must be the fairest in the sea!"

"Perhaps another time," said my aunt. "We have something we have to do first."

Since the witch was busy with her shells, it was easy to sneak away. I glanced at Grassina. The worried look on her face frightened me. "That was Cadmilla, one of the most devious witches around. Everyone knows that she tried to kill her stepdaughter."

"But she seemed nice, too!" I said.

Grassina shook her head. "It doesn't make any sense, does it? If even their personalities have changed—"

"They must have lost their memories altogether,"

said Eadric, digging the toe of his boot into the sand.

"Eadric!" I said, startled at his brilliance. "I bet that's it!"

"It makes sense, doesn't it? They can't even remember their own names, let alone who Grassina or Olivene are. If they can't remember that much, there's probably a lot they can't remember."

Shading my eyes with my hand, I glanced down the beach. "We'll just have to look for Grandmother. She must be around here somewhere."

We finally found my grandmother lying on a blanket, sound asleep. Her face was relaxed, without the cruel lines that usually etched her skin, and she looked kind of sweet lying there. I almost didn't recognize her.

"Do you think we should wake her?" I whispered to my aunt. "She looks so peaceful."

"What's all this noise about?" said my grandmother, turning her head to glare at us.

My aunt looked defiant, which was the way she usually acted around her mother. "We came to find you."

"Why? Do I know you? Doesn't matter. I'm taking a nap. Go bother someone else." My grandmother rolled onto her side, turning her back to us. Perhaps it was the curse, but even without her memory, Grandmother was the nastiest witch around.

Grassina shook her head and walked away, gesturing for me to follow. "This may take a while," she said once we were out of my grandmother's earshot. "Why don't you and Eadric see what else you can learn about the island? The more we know, the sooner we can get your grandmother's memory back and ask her to reverse the spell on Haywood."

"Will we take Grandmother with us when we go?" I asked.

"That depends on what we learn. Just be careful. There's more going on here than you might imagine."

Seven

Eadric and I headed down the beach in the only direction we had yet to explore. Although we didn't see anyone, we did spot a lone hut set off by itself. Larger than the others, it had the same cone-shaped thatched roof and stick-built walls, and it was situated on a small spit of land that overlooked the beach on one side and a tree-lined bay on the other.

As we got closer, we could tell that something was going on inside the hut. A shrill, scratchy voice was screaming, "Me too! Me too!" A deeper, less distinct voice answered.

Although it was broad daylight, with all the greenery we were able to sneak up and peek inside without anyone noticing. I saw only one person, a short old man with white hair, a rounded belly, a substantial mustache and a neat, trim beard. Dressed in a knee-length light blue robe, the old man wore a soft, four-cornered cap that threatened to slip off each time he turned his head. Both robe and cap were decorated with scattered silver stars, and a chain of larger stars twinkled around his neck. A large green and red bird with a well-developed beak sat on a perch beside him.

On a table against the wall, pink and white seashells held down the edges of a fresh piece of parchment. A quill pen lay on the table, dripping ink beside a small clay pot. From where I crouched, I could see that the parchment was clean except for a few written words and a splattering of ink.

"I'm sick and tired of this!" grumbled the old man.

"Me too!" squawked the bird, shuffling back and forth on its perch.

"I can't wait until we're finished and can go home."

"Me too!"

"I wish you'd think of something else to say!"

"Me too!"

The wizard's left eyelid twitched. "You know, it was funny at first, but now it's just annoying. Stop saying 'Me too,' Metoo!"

"*Thppt!*" The bird made a rude sound with its beak.

"Now cut that out! I don't know why I put up with you."

"Grack!" said the bird.

The old man shook a pudgy pink finger. "You stupid bird. If it weren't for you, we would have been finished and out of here already!"

"Awk!" squawked the bird. "Don't blame me, Olefat! I told you that lying to a bunch of old witches would get you in trouble, but you had to steal their memories—"

"It seemed like a good idea," said Olefat. "All those memories just waiting to be bottled up. Once I found the book, it was only a matter of time."

"You wouldn't have needed to do it if you could come up with your own spells."

Olefat shook his head. "That wasn't the point. Those witches were once the leaders in their field. By collecting their spells, I'm doing the world of magic a service."

"Then don't come crying to me when you don't like what you hear. Even you couldn't have expected those old memories to be pleasant." Sidling along his perch, the bird twisted his head to the side to stare at the old wizard.

"I never thought they'd be this bad," Olefat wailed. "I can't stand much more!"

Something rattled, and I peeked over the window ledge to see what it was. A row of bottles filled a shelf that had been pegged to the opposite wall. One bottle was a sickly yellow shot through with violet; another was gray with purple specks the color of a bruise. While some bottles were shaking, one that was the color of dried blood looked like it was about to rattle itself completely off the shelf.

"Are you through yet?" said a scratchy voice. "I'm sick of hearing you two yammer on. Close your mouths and listen before I turn you into a couple of cockroaches!"

"You're so full of hot air!" said another voice, shriller than the first. "You can't cast spells now. You're just a memory."

"Quiet, you old crones. It's my turn and I'm going to have my say. Ahem," said a husky voice clearing a nonexistent throat. "I married a widower king who doted on me for my beauty. I kept my splendor for years with a lotion I made from the dust of a thousand butterfly wings and the milk from two bushels of milkweed pods. I was very happy for a time, since I was the fairest in the land. But then my stepdaughter turned sixteen and ruined it all by being even more beautiful."

"A thousand butterfly wings..." muttered the old man as he scribbled on the piece of parchment.

Another witch cackled. "You wasted your life trying to stay beautiful while I spent my days teaching lessons to those who deserved it. Every day I waited for someone to come into my woods. If a maid shared her lunch with me, I cast a spell so that each time she spoke, pearls and precious gems fell from her lips. Maids who refused to share their food had frogs, snakes and lizards squirming from their throats."

"What if it was a gentleman instead of a maid?" asked the old man.

"Generous gentlemen received swords of valor or enchanted cloaks. As for the stingy ones—"

A familiar voice broke in. "I transformed people as well, but not always for being selfish. I changed my daughter's betrothed into an otter because I didn't think he was good enough for her. When I told him how to break the spell, I made it so involved that he was bound to forget it."

"Is that your grandmother?" Eadric whispered into my ear.

I nodded, shushing him with a raised finger.

"So tell us what you said!" demanded one voice.

"I don't think I will. It was too delicious!"

Go ahead, I thought. *Tell them!*

"That isn't fair! I told you my recipe for beauty."

"We won't share anything else with you if you don't share with us."

"Oh, all right, if you're going to be that way. I remember it word for word, since it was so perfect."

A gossamer hair from mother-of-pearl,
The breath of a dragon green.
A feather from an aged horse,
The husk of a magic bean.

70

"I see what you mean. He couldn't possibly have gotten that right."

"It wasn't impossible, mind you, or it wouldn't have worked."

"But for an otter to remember that, or find half the things—"

"How long did he stay an otter?"

"As far as I know, he still is!" screeched my grandmother.

The hoots of laughter from the bottles made me so angry, I felt like shaking them.

"Now it's my turn!" screamed a voice over the din. "And have I got a story."

"Who said you could go next? You talked yesterday, so it's my turn."

I backed away from the window, tugging on Eadric's sleeve. "It's time for us to go," I whispered. "We've heard what we came for."

"But it's just getting good!" he whispered a little too loudly.

"What was that?" asked the bird. "I think I heard something."

"You're always hearing something," the wizard replied. "It's probably a loose seed rattling around in your skull."

The bird's outraged squawk hurt my ears. "Loose seeds! I'll give you loose seeds!" *Plip! Plip! Plip!* The last thing I saw through the window before I started to run was the bird flinging seeds at the old man.

We found Grassina seated on the blanket beside my grandmother, who had fallen asleep again. Haywood was chasing seagulls up and down the beach, and appeared to be having a wonderful time.

"We found the answer!" I said. "You have to come with us."

"There's a little old wizard named Olefat—" began Eadric, shifting his weight from one foot to the other.

Grassina stood and brushed the sand from her gown. "Olefat? I didn't know he was still alive. It's been years since I've heard anyone mention his name. I'm not surprised he's involved," she said, looking grim. "He has a shady reputation."

"He's the one behind all this," said Eadric. "You should see his hut. He put the memories in bottles and keeps them on a shelf."

Grassina began walking and we hurried to catch up. "He has the memories with him now?" she asked, a determined glint in her eyes. "Are you sure?"

"We heard them ourselves!" said Eadric. "He was arguing with a bird. It's the size of a crow, but it's green and red and has a much bigger beak."

"That sounds like a parrot."

"And then other voices started talking," I said. "They called themselves memories, but they weren't very nice."

Grassina shook her head. "No, they wouldn't be. A nasty group of witches lives in that retirement community. Maybe all the nice ones moved away— or never moved there in the first place, once they'd learned who already lived there. Not all old witches are nasty."

"That's good," said Eadric, smiling at me. He pointed at the hut down the beach. "We listened through the window and we heard your—"

Grassina held up her hand for silence. "You two did very well, but I think you'd better stay outside. It may get unpleasant in there."

Once again Eadric and I crouched beneath Olefat's window. Hearing my aunt knock on the door, I peeked over the sill, careful to stay out of sight. The old wizard looked startled.

"Who do you suppose that is?" Olefat asked his parrot.

The parrot squawked and threw another seed at him. "You're the wizard. You tell me!"

Olefat took off his hat, trickling seeds on the floor. His head was bald but for a fringe of hair that reached from ear to ear. Frowning, he rubbed his bald spot before jamming his cap back on his head. "Come in," he called, his eyelid twitching so much, it looked like a living thing trying to escape.

When Grassina opened the door, all the blood

drained from Olefat's face. Muttering under his breath, he began to reach into a fold in his robe, but Grassina threw up her hand and pointed her finger at him.

No word, no gesture shall you make!
Silence keep for your life's sake!

Olefat's mouth flew open, and it seemed as though he was about to speak. When nothing came out, his eyes took on a wild look. His jaw waggled, and his Adam's apple jerked up and down.

The parrot squawked, bobbing its head like a broken child's toy. "Would you look at that? That's the first time I've seen the old man speechless. You should have come by sooner. Why, we—"

Grassina pursed her lips and narrowed her eyes, a look that too often meant that someone was in trouble. "Silence, bird, or you'll never speak again," she said. The parrot's beak closed with a snap.

Grassina nodded, apparently satisfied. "Now let's get down to business." Pointing her finger at the old man once more, she recited a truthfulness spell.

Let the truth be known to all.
No more tales—short or tall.
May the words we need to hear
Pass from your lips to waiting ear.

From this day on, the truth you'll tell.
There's just one way to break the spell.
Three selfless acts you must perform
To aid a stranger who's forlorn.

It was a spell I'd heard before. Only a few months earlier a knight had boasted that he was responsible for the death of a dragon terrorizing a neighboring kingdom. When someone questioned the knight's story, Grassina was called in to verify the truth. It was an important point, for whoever had killed the dragon would win the hand of the princess and get half the kingdom. It turned out that a groom in the king's stable had really been responsible, which pleased the princess, for he was younger and much better-looking than the knight. The truth would probably never have come out if it hadn't been for Grassina.

As my aunt finished the spell, Olefat's eyes grew large and his hands began to shake. I wondered if he had heard of the spell and knew what it really meant. "You may talk now," said Grassina, "but I must say that you should be ashamed of yourself. It wasn't the first time you've done something like this, I warrant."

"No, I've done the same thing before." Even while he spoke, a look of horror altered Olefat's features. Stepping back, he clapped both hands over his mouth.

"Tell me, how did you get their memories?"

Olefat shook his head, but it didn't do him any good, for the words spilled out no matter what he did. "I bought a book from a merchant who didn't know what he was selling. Most of the spells were useless, but I tried the memory spell and it worked. I'm terrible at coming up with spells on my own, so I thought this was the perfect way to get some good ones."

The parrot squawked and flicked another seed at Olefat. "Stop talking, you idiot! You're going to tell her everything! Haven't you gotten us in enough trouble already?"

"I can't help it!" Olefat wailed.

Grassina's glance shifted from the parrot back to Olefat. "How did you get the ladies to come to the island?"

"I lied. I told them that I'd found some great swampland that was selling for next to nothing. When I gave them pictures, they wanted to leave right away."

"How did you get them all here?"

"That spell was in the book, too. The witches needed something as a focus, so I gave them bags of sand. I linked their brooms with a spell and took their memories the moment they landed."

Grassina nodded, as if something she'd suspected had just been confirmed. "Where is this book now?"

"Don't tell her, you idiot!" screeched the parrot.

Olefat struggled to keep his mouth closed, squeezing

his lips shut with his fingers. When he tried to speak anyway, his words were indistinguishable. Grassina sighed and reached out to pinch his nose so that he was forced to breathe through his mouth. The old man held out as long as he could, but when his face started to turn blue, he let go of his lips, gasped once and blurted out, "It's in the chest under the table!"

"Aagh!" shrieked the parrot. "Now you've done it, you old fool!"

Olefat began to weep enormous tears. When Grassina started toward the table, the parrot let out an earsplitting screech and flew at her in a flurry of beak and claws. I sensed movement beside me, and a furry body catapulted through the window. Although I hadn't known that Haywood had joined us, he seemed to know exactly what was going on. In a flash, he tackled the bird and had it pinned to the floor. The bird beat its wings in his face and tried to bite him, but I guess the otter was used to uncooperative food, for he knew how to hold it without getting hurt.

"Haywood, my darling, be careful!" Grassina said.

"I'm fine, my sweet," the otter assured her before turning back to the bird. Pressing down on the thrashing parrot, he said, "If you don't stop that right now, I'll rip off your beak and stuff it down your scruffy little throat."

The parrot's beak closed with a snap, and it jerked its

wings to its sides. "You wouldn't dare," said the parrot.

Haywood smiled grimly at the bird. "Try me."

"What's going on out there?" demanded a memory. "Who is that?"

"I heard my daughter Grassina," said my grandmother's voice. "I'd recognize the ungrateful wretch's voice anywhere."

My aunt's lip curled as if she'd tasted something foul. "Hello, Mother. If you don't mind, I'm a little busy now."

"What difference would it make if I did mind? My feelings never mattered to you before. But don't worry. I'll shut up and let you go about your important business, Lady High and Mighty!"

Ignoring the other memories who continued to mutter among themselves, my aunt raised the lid of the trunk and reached inside. When she sat back, she held a small brown volume in her hand. "Is this the book?" she asked, holding it up for Olefat to see.

The old man nodded, sniffling into his sleeve. His whole body seemed to slump.

"Good," she said, tucking the book into her pouch. "Then you won't be needing it anymore."

"In a way I'm glad someone showed up," said Olefat, wiping the tears from his cheeks. "Those old witches' memories were driving me crazy. You never met a nastier bunch of women. When I think about all the effort I put into this without getting much real information... They could gossip all right, and they loved to brag, but getting them to describe their actual spells—"

"Gossip?" shrilled a memory. "Did you hear that, ladies? The old geezer called us gossips! Just wait till we get our hands on you, you old—"

"You don't have hands!" Olefat said, smiling through his tears.

Grassina sighed and shook her head. "How do I return the memories to their owners?"

"Break the bottles," Olefat answered, gasping when he realized what he'd said. "But please, if you have any decency in you, let me go first. Those old bats would love to tear me apart!"

"After what you've done, that might be exactly what you deserve."

With an anguished groan, the old man fell to his knees and raised clasped hands to my aunt. "Please, I beg you, let me go!"

"Get up, old man, and get out of here. But you'd better hurry because I'm about to break every bottle in the room. These are all the bottles, aren't they?"

"Every one is on that shelf!"

Grassina reached toward a bottle. "Are you still here?" she asked Olefat.

"No! No, wait!" The old man moved faster than I thought possible. "Come along, Metoo," he said, snatching the parrot from Haywood. With the bird tucked under one arm, Olefat dragged the trunk out from under the table and climbed inside. The parrot hissed at the otter while the old man cast one last glance around the room before slamming the lid shut. I heard him mutter something, then the trunk began to move, rising off the floor and gliding out the door as smoothly as grease on water, passing Eadric and me on its way to the ocean.

Eight

As soon as Olefat was gone, Eadric and I hurried into the hut. We joined Grassina at the window to watch the trunk skim the tops of the waves. "That spell should put a crimp in his style, shouldn't it?" said Eadric.

"I hope so," said Grassina. She carried a black and green bottle to the window, where direct sunlight made it look diseased. "It almost seems a shame to let these go. The old witches are much nicer without their memories." Gesturing toward the shelf, she said, "Would you two like to help me with the bottles?"

Eadric grinned. "How can we resist?"

"I'll wait outside," said Haywood, and blew Grassina a kiss. "I'd just be in the way now."

"Thank you for all your help, my darling," called Grassina as the otter scurried out the door. "You were wonderful!"

We took turns smashing the bottles against the back wall, throwing them one at a time. As each bottle broke, the memories fled the hut in greasy, multicolored swirls. When all the bottles were broken, Eadric and I followed Grassina through the door, surprised to find that the sun was setting. We passed an angry group plotting their revenge on Olefat. Three witches had already set off in pursuit of the wizard.

We were crossing the beach when Haywood trotted over to join us. "Can we talk to your mother now?" he asked my aunt.

Grassina reached down to fondle his ears. "If we can find her. She may have left already."

We spotted my grandmother inspecting her broom near one of the huts. She had changed back into the black gown and pointy-toed shoes she normally wore.

"Mother, I need to speak with you," announced Grassina.

Grandmother swung around and glared at my aunt. "What is it? I'm in a hurry."

Slipping past Grassina, Haywood sat back on his haunches and stared up at my grandmother. "Hello, Olivene. Remember me?"

"By the breath of a cross-eyed bat, if it isn't that good-for-nothing Henley. So you finally found him, did you, Grassina? It took you longer than I thought it would, but then you always were a little slow. Tell me, daughter, what is he doing here?"

"Haywood and I still love each other, and we want to get married."

"So what's stopping you?"

Grassina sighed. "I've come to ask you to reverse the spell and turn Haywood back into a man. It's the least you can do since I saved your memory from Olefat."

Grandmother glanced at Haywood, who had chosen that moment to scrub his face with a paw. "You want a man, do you? There are enough men out there to pick from."

"But I want Haywood!"

This wasn't going at all the way I thought it would. Grandmother was supposed to be thankful and reasonable. Haywood was supposed to act less like an otter and more like a man. And Grassina wasn't supposed to lose her temper.

"Grandmother," I said, hoping to set things right, "I suggested they come. I know how much you've wanted more grandchildren, and I thought if they got married—"

"Why would I want another grandchild? The one I have is the greatest disappointment of my life! You refuse to follow the family trade, you let your mother bully you and you've never given a thought to what you want to do with yourself. When I was your age, I knew exactly what I wanted to do and I did it! You think everything should be handed to you on a platter, but life doesn't work that way. If you cared about your family, you'd live up to your responsibilities and learn to be a witch!"

"That isn't fair! I actually—"

"And as for you," she said, rounding on Grassina. "I may be old, but I haven't forgotten why I turned Horace into an otter in the first place. He doesn't have the talent the way you do. He comes from a family whose witches can't make a decent potion without reading it from a book. Forget about him. He's wasting your time and talents." With a wave of her hand and some foreign-sounding words, Grandmother gestured toward Haywood, who disappeared with an audible pop.

"Haywood!" screamed Grassina, her eyes wide with horror as she stared at the empty spot where the otter had just stood. "Mother, what have you done?"

"I've done you both a favor by sending him to a very nice place where he should be perfectly happy, if he survives. He's going to start forgetting you, Grassina. By the third day, he'll have forgotten that he was ever human. An hour after the sun rises on the fourth day, the change will be permanent. Now get out of my way. That half-baked wizard Olefat has a lot to answer for, and I'm going to make sure he has a miserable time doing it." Twirling her cloak around her shoulders, Grandmother swung her leg over her broom and leaned forward. Before my grandmother could take off, however,

Grassina darted in front of her and grabbed the broom handle.

"No, you don't, Mother!" Grassina said. "You're not leaving until you bring my Haywood back!" I had never seen my aunt so angry before. Her face was red and veins stood out on her forehead.

"Out of my way, you ninny!" screeched my grandmother. "It's not my fault that you're too dim-witted to know when someone's done you a good turn." She flicked her fingers at Grassina. Silver sparks shot from her fingertips, sizzling like fat on a hot pan. A spark landed on Grassina's wrist, burning her skin.

Grassina jumped back, gesturing with both hands while muttering something under her breath. A swirl of snowflakes whispered between the two women, extinguishing sparks with a hiss. When the snow cleared, my grandmother had already shot into the sky, cackling that nasty laugh of hers. "Horatio's not good enough for you, Grassina!" she screeched. "Forget about him!"

"That horrible witch!" exclaimed Grassina, scowling at my grandmother as she flew out of sight. "She can't do this to me again. I won't let her get away with it!"

I shook sparks from my skirt and resolved that I would never use my magic to hurt anyone. It hadn't occurred to me that my grandmother would try to hurt her own daughter.

"Now what am I going to do?" wailed my aunt.

"Even if I bring Haywood home before four days are up, Mother will refuse to change him back."

"You don't need her to do it! Eadric tried to tell you earlier—we overheard her explain to the other memories what you need to reverse it."

> A gossamer hair from mother-of-pearl,
> The breath of a dragon green.
> A feather from an aged horse,
> The husk of a magic bean.

Tears streamed down Grassina's face. I couldn't remember ever seeing my aunt cry before. "But I have to find Haywood!" she said. "I'm sure she sent him somewhere ghastly. I don't have time to find him *and* all those items."

"All you have to do is find Haywood," I said. "Eadric and I can start looking for the things you need. We'll meet you back at the castle. Today is Tuesday, so four days from now would be Saturday. If we work together, I'm sure we can do this."

"I don't know if I should let you," said Grassina. "It may be too dangerous. You'd need to look in the sea for the mother-of-pearl, and as to getting the dragon's breath—"

"That part should be easy. I already know where we can find a dragon. We came across one in the enchanted forest."

"I don't think—"

"Please, Grassina. It's my fault that you talked to Grandmother. If I hadn't been so sure that she would help us, we'd all be back at the castle right now and none of this would have happened. Please let me make it up to you. I can do this, I know I can."

"I can't—"

"You've helped me my whole life, and this is the first time I'll be able to do something for you. Please give me the chance."

Grassina wiped tears from her eyes with the back of her hand. "Are you sure about this? It won't be easy."

Eadric interrupted. "Of course we'll do it. Emma is your only niece, and I keep hoping that someday …" He put his arm around my shoulders.

"Then I suppose …" My aunt smiled feebly and reached for our hands. We took her hands in ours and held them tightly. "Thank you, Emma, Eadric," she said. "You don't know what this means to me. I need to go after Haywood before his trail gets cold. You may use the magic carpet, of course. I'll have it take you directly home. I already know where you can find the first item. Emma, open the silver chest in my bedchamber. Take the silver comb to the saltwater bowl. Run the comb through your hair three times, then do the same for Eadric. Put the comb in your pouch—keep it safe, for you'll need it to come back—and dip your hand in the salt water. This will take you into the sea, but don't worry, you'll be fine. When you get to the castle, ask for my friend Coral. She's a sea witch and she'll help you all she can. Be sure to take her a gift. When I come home, I'll get whatever you haven't located."

"How will you find Haywood without the carpet?"

"I have my ways." Sticking two fingers in her mouth, Grassina whistled, then turned back to me. "Tell your mother what your grandmother did. You can also tell her that she doesn't need to worry. I'll be home soon. Now climb on and be careful," she said as the carpet landed at our feet.

"How do you steer it?" I asked.

My aunt seemed edgy and impatient to go. She sighed and said, "I don't have time to show you now. It already knows the way home, so you won't have to worry about steering. Just say 'home' and it will do the rest."

Eadric and I looked at each other. He swallowed hard and said, "I'm ready when you are."

I nodded and tried not to think about falling off. Clenching my teeth, I stepped onto the carpet and sat down, taking deep breaths to calm my pounding heart. I was trying to get comfortable when my hand brushed the pouch hanging from my belt. "Maybe this could help," I said, taking out the string. "If I could turn this into some sort of strap to hold us on—"

"Emma, you clever girl! That's a marvelous idea."

Grassina's eyes lit up, and I realized that she was more worried about us than she let show. She gestured, and the string grew into a heavy cord that whipped around my waist, attaching itself to the carpet behind me.

I glanced at Eadric, who was secured as well. Although it wasn't much, it made me feel better. *Stay calm,* I told myself, closing my eyes as the carpet began to rise.

Nine

The flight back to the castle was nothing like our trip to the island. After I told the carpet, "home," it rotated until it faced the right direction and took off at a smooth and steady pace into the darkening sky. Eadric and I were tense at first, waiting for the ride to become bumpy or the carpet to suddenly go limp. When the flight remained uneventful, we both began to relax.

"You didn't ask me if I wanted to go," said Eadric, "but I really want to help you find those things for Grassina. She helped us break the spell and gave me back my life. I owe her, so I'm honor-bound to do whatever it takes to get her and Haywood together again. Anything less would be unworthy of a prince."

"I don't see how—"

"Anyway, I've been thinking about the things we have to find. Grassina said that her friend will help us locate the gossamer hair, and even I've heard of magic beans, so they can't be that hard to get. The feather of an aged horse might be tricky. I've never seen a horse with feathers, so I don't know how we'll handle that one. Your aunt will probably know what to do when she comes home. You were wrong about the dragons, though. It isn't going to be quick and easy, as you seem to think. 'The breath of a dragon green.'" Eadric shook his head. "It's too bad we don't have the vial I lugged around when I was a frog. That dragon's breath had lots of colors in it, and one of them must have been green. You don't suppose we could go find the swamp fairy and ask if we can have it back?"

"Even if we could find that fairy, and even if she agreed to give it back, there's no guarantee that the dragon who breathed into that vial was green. Breath of a dragon green isn't the same as green breath of a dragon. I think we're going to have to find a green dragon and get its breath somehow."

"I've had a few run-ins with dragons," said Eadric, "and they all have nasty tempers. Even when we find one, we can't just ask it to breathe into a vial. I'm going to need a new sword. I lost my old one in the swamp when that witch turned me into a frog. All I've got now is my dagger, and that's not nearly enough if I'm going to face a dragon. I've been thinking about that, too. Killing a dragon isn't so hard, but collecting its breath while it's still alive ..." Eadric tapped his chin. "I suppose I could do it if the beast was asleep."

"Then that's our solution. I'll have a sleeping spell ready when—"

Eadric scowled. "I thought we'd get a sleeping potion."

"What would you do, toss the dragon meat laced with your potion and hope it eats the meat before it eats you?"

"I'd sooner do that than depend on your magic!" Eadric said. "For all I know, you'd put *us* to sleep instead of the dragon!"

"I'll have you know that my magic is getting better!"

"Oh, really? You already turned me into an old man with your magic, remember? I'll take my chances with a potion, if you don't mind. I'd rather you didn't come up with any more spells for a while. I think we'd both be better off without them."

"I didn't know you felt that way!"

"I didn't know you could be so stubborn!"

Eadric was right in a way. My magic wasn't very good yet, and it did complicate things. I didn't seem to be having any problems with the spells I read, only the ones I came up with myself. Grassina had told me to keep working on my magic, but maybe I should have just concentrated on learning the established spells. I seemed to have a good memory for spells, even though I'd never been very adept at remembering other things, like the social niceties my mother wanted me to learn.

The rest of the trip was spent in cold, miserable silence. I dozed for a time, coming fully awake as dawn was breaking behind the Purple Mountains. Although shrouded in mist, they were a lovely and welcome sight. Eadric woke when the carpet entered the tower window; the funny popping sound it made when the window widened was loud enough to wake the ghosts in the dungeon. The straps came undone as soon as we landed, slipping off us like an insult off an ogre. It felt good to have solid footing, and I bent and stretched, trying to work the kinks out of my legs and back.

Still refusing to talk to me, Eadric headed straight for the castle kitchen, but I wanted to say hello to Li'l first. I found her in the storage room, hanging from a rafter.

"So, there you are!" she said, sounding delighted to see me. "I heard you come in. Quick, tell me everything that happened."

I did, and I finished with the list of items we needed to transform Haywood. As it was Wednesday morning, we didn't have much time, so we'd have to go see Grassina's friend Coral as soon as we could. "And Grassina said that I should find a gift for the sea witch. Do you have any ideas?"

Li'l tilted her head and looked thoughtful. "I'd be happy to help, but I'm going to need time to think. Why don't you get something to eat before you scare everybody in the castle? Your stomach sounds like a dragon

93

having a bad dream."

As I was leaving Grassina's apartment, I nearly ran into Eadric. He was juggling a tottering platter heaped high with cold roast duck, boiled partridge eggs, thick slices of dark bread and chunks of yellow cheese. "Hey!" he said. "What's the hurry?"

"I was heading to the kitchen."

He eyed the pile of food. "Good, then get me a couple more—"

Someone must have opened the door at the bottom of the steps, for suddenly the stairwell was flooded with noise. Because of the way the castle was constructed, anyone standing on the stairs could hear even the faintest sounds in the Great Hall when the connecting door was open. It sounded as if a large crowd had gathered and everyone was talking at once. Since one of the more distinctive voices was my mother's, I knew I probably couldn't avoid running into her if I went to the kitchen. I took my time going down the stairs while I thought about what I would say, scarcely noticing Eadric as he continued the list of food he wanted me to bring him.

Reaching the bottom of the steps, I saw that the Great Hall was bustling with servants, soldiers and courtiers. When I stepped into the room, I spotted my mother speaking with the castle steward. A short distance away, my father stood listening to the captain of the guard, who excused himself when he noticed me approaching.

"Father!" I said, pleased to see him. I would have liked it if he had opened his arms to me for a hug, but that was not his way. Skirting a trio of ladies-in-waiting, I bobbed my head to my mother, then hurried past her to my father's side. His smile was genuine, but the circles under his eyes and the weary stoop to his shoulders concerned me. My father was tall, with broad shoulders and blond hair turning to gray. A strong man, he feared little, so when I saw him looking worried, I worried as well.

"Your mother told me what happened to you," he said. "You must learn to be more careful."

"Of course, Father." I decided to postpone telling him about my latest adventures.

"Where is Grassina?" my mother asked, coming up from behind me. "I have to speak to her right away. Is she still upstairs?" Mother glanced toward the stairwell as if expecting my aunt to come down at any moment.

I shook my head. "She's not here. It was awful! When we asked Grandmother to help us, she refused, then banished Haywood to the wilderness. Grassina's gone to look for him. She said that you shouldn't worry."

Mother looked upset. "Of course I'll worry. Everything has gone wrong since she left. Limelyn, tell Emeralda about the spies."

The creases in my father's brow deepened. "All we

learned was that King Beltran had sent them to watch our family."

"Isn't King Beltran Prince Jorge's father?" I asked.

"Yes, unfortunately," said my mother. "I thought that if we made an alliance between our two countries, Beltran would leave us alone. He's coveted our western land for years. Your aunt Grassina's reputation for magic is the only reason he hasn't tried to take it by force."

My father nodded. "After we discovered Beltran's spies, I sent my own to his kingdom. I've just received their report. Jorge learned about your disappearance and thought that you had run away so you wouldn't have to marry him. When you returned with Prince Eadric, Jorge was convinced that he was right and swears that he no longer wants to marry you. Despite his son's wishes, Beltran plans to force the wedding. He's telling everyone that you and Jorge were officially betrothed and that you signed all the documents. I'm to give him half my western lands as your dowry."

"But that's ridiculous!" I exclaimed. "I never signed any documents, and there was no betrothal ceremony! And to demand that you give up land—"

"That's all he really wants. The rest is just an excuse," Mother said through clenched teeth. "I wouldn't let you marry that horrible man's son now for all the dust in East Aridia!"

"Beltran knows that the only way he'd get our land is

through force. He's called his men to arms," Father continued. "His spies have told him that Grassina is away, so he may well believe he has the opening he needs."

"This is the worst possible time for her to be running around in the wilderness," said my mother. "Greater Greensward has been at peace for centuries, although that could change if your aunt isn't here to use her magic. War can do horrible things to a kingdom."

I was puzzled. "How could Beltran's spies have told him about Grassina so quickly? She's been gone only a day."

"From the way they escaped, we think that at least one of the spies was a wizard," said my father. "They turned into birds and flew away."

My mother frowned. "That's why we need your aunt back here now. Your father is perfectly capable of dealing with any ordinary army. However, if Beltran has magic at his disposal, we need magic of our own."

"What can I do?"

"There really isn't anything—" Mother started.

"Please, Mother, there must be some way I can help. You've always said that I should take more interest in my duties as a princess."

"Very well, then. See if you can get Grassina home and focused on her work. She can't waste any more time on Haywood when she has a job to do here."

"I'll see what I can do. I already know what she needs

97

to turn Haywood back. Eadric and I are going to collect the items and—"

"Is he still here?" asked my mother. "Doesn't that boy have a home? It's bad enough that he ruined your reputation. Now we can't get rid of him. My steward has been complaining about him, too. It seems your Prince Eadric eats more than three knights."

"He's already been a big help—" I began.

My mother laughed. "I can't imagine how."

"And I'd be able to help Grassina better if Eadric was helping me."

Mother sighed. "I suppose he may stay, but only as long as he's being helpful."

"Has the young man given you any indication regarding his intentions toward you?" asked my father.

"He says he wants to marry me." I really hadn't wanted to tell my parents until I'd made up my mind, but I didn't want to lie about it, either.

"Perhaps it's his sense of chivalry that is making him say that," said my mother. "He must know that he's sullied your good name."

"I don't think that's it at all. I'm sure—"

My mother snorted, making a most unladylike sound. "You can't believe that he offered because he has feelings for you, Emeralda. You're too willful to make a good wife, and you're neither dainty nor delicate, as a princess should be. Heaven knows I've done what I could with you, but even I could only do so much. Since he's made an offer, however, my hard work must have had some effect."

If I didn't do something to stop her, my mother would be making wedding plans before I was even engaged. "I didn't accept his offer," I said.

Mother gasped. "What? I didn't realize that you were this foolish! His offer may be the only one you'll receive!"

"I didn't turn Eadric down; I just didn't say yes. I told him I'd have to think about it."

My mother's face was turning red. "This is preposterous. You should have jumped at the chance to …" She caught herself, and a slow smile softened her mouth. "No, wait, perhaps you're wiser than I realized. Sometimes playing hard to get—"

"I wasn't playing hard to get. I just don't know if I want to marry him."

"And that's exactly why you need your father and me, young lady," said my mother. "Without our guidance, you'd end up a pitiful old spinster like your aunt Grassina, and we would end up giving the country to relatives we don't even like."

I bit back the angry reply that burned in my throat. My aunt was far from pitiful and was only a few years older than my mother. Trying to look meeker than I felt, I thanked my parents for their advice and hurried to the kitchen, collected a hunk of bread and some cheese and left through the back door.

Eadric was still eating when I reached Grassina's rooms. He smiled at me, and I could tell that having food in his stomach had put him in a better mood, although he seemed a bit disappointed that I hadn't brought him more. While he nibbled a piece of duck, I told him about King Beltran and how he wanted to force me to marry Jorge.

Eadric's eyebrows shot up. "That's terrible!" he said. "He can't do that. You're going to marry me!"

"Jorge no longer wants to marry me, but my parents said that his father wants our western lands."

"I'll tell your father that I'll fight at his side. I know we aren't officially betrothed—"

"They said that the best thing we can do is help Grassina. They need her back here with her magic at full strength, and that means we have to help her take care of Haywood."

"Then that's what we'll do, but as soon as we've finished, I'm joining your father."

"I know he'd appreciate your help," I said. "You two will probably get along well together. You both enjoy a lot of the same things. My mother's a different story, though. Unless she decides that she likes you, she can be very unpleasant."

"Then I'll just have to get her to like me," Eadric

said, popping another egg in his mouth with greasy fingers.

"I hope you have better luck at that than I have. Even though she's my mother, I don't think she ever really liked me. But you have one factor in your favor that I never had—you're a boy."

While Eadric finished eating, I excused myself and went into the storage room to look for a gift for Coral. Li'l was inside, perched atop an old, dusty trunk that reminded me of Olefat's, except this one was in much sadder shape. Battered and dented, its surface was covered with grainy and badly pitted dark green leather. I couldn't understand why anyone would choose a hide of this type.

"What is that?" I asked, running my hand over the uneven surface.

"I asked your aunt that same question," said Li'l. "She said it's the skin off a troll's backside." Grimacing, I snatched my hand away and rubbed it on my skirt. "It's supposed to be tough and last a long time. That's the trunk your grandmother gave Grassina when the old woman retired. I thought we could look inside for a gift for that sea witch, although I have a few other things we could look at if there's nothing in there. Lift the lid and we'll take a peek. It's too heavy for me."

The little bat fluttered to the top of the magic mirror propped against the wall, leaving me standing by the trunk. Gritting my teeth, I grabbed hold of the lid and shoved.

It opened with the groan of ancient hinges, and I imagined that it was the voice of the long-dead troll. Kneeling on the floor, I reached into the shadowy recesses and began to take items out one at a time while Li'l named the things she recognized.

A ridged tooth as long as my thumb dangled from a golden chain. Li'l gasped, claiming it was from a manticore. The stiff gray hairs tied with silver thread were bundled werewolf whiskers. An ancient jar of yellow, crusty flakes was a collection of goblin earwax. Another jar held jagged black crescents that Li'l identified as nail clippings from an ogre. The little bat hissed when I held up a jar containing coarse, stringy hair caked with something brown and glossy. Shuddering, Li'l told me that it was the hair from a harpy and could empty even the largest castle with its stench.

I had just set the jar back in the trunk when Eadric stepped into the room. "Find anything yet?" he asked.

"Nothing we'd want to give anyone." I closed the lid of the trunk before he could dig around inside. "Li'l, didn't you say that you might have some other things?"

"There's the golden feather from the golden goose, but I don't think you'll want to take that. It has golden bird lice on it," Li'l said. "They're a pretty color, but they sure do tickle."

"And that's it?" I asked.

"There is something else in a little box behind the mirror, but I don't think you'll want it, either."

I found the box easily enough. When I opened the lid, there was only one thing inside: a silver hairpin with a ruby head shaped like a fish. "What's wrong with it, Li'l? Was it dipped in poison? Does it make the wearer sleep forever or turn her into a fish? What does it do?"

"That's just it. It doesn't do anything."

"So why wouldn't I want to take it?"

"Because it doesn't have any magic. I thought you wanted something special, and that pin is boring."

"A fish-shaped ruby is perfect for a mermaid! Since she's a magical being, she probably has all sorts of magical things already. We'll take the pin. I'm sure she'll like it." The box was too big to fit in my pouch, so I took the pin out and pushed it through the fabric of my sleeve until I was sure it was secure.

I had turned around to show Eadric when I heard Li'l exclaim, "What's that? Is it alive?"

"What are you talking about?" I asked.

"There, in the back," said Li'l, pointing at my gown with her wing.

I grabbed the back of my skirt and pulled it around to get a better look. I didn't see anything unusual until Eadric reached down and plucked something from my hem.

"Would you look at this!" he said, holding up a little

green crab identical to those we'd seen on the island.

I bent down for a closer look. "How did that get there?"

I'd thought the island crabs couldn't talk, so I was surprised when the little creature spoke. "I saw you change from a green hopping thing into a human," the crab said in a scratchy voice. "I wanted to see you do it again so I could learn how to do it, too. I've been holding on ever since you walked past. My claws are tired!"

"I can't show you how to turn into a human," I said. "I was a human before I was a frog, and I was just turning back. I've never heard of an animal turning into a human."

"I have," said Li'l, "but it hardly ever works out. Life as a human is too confusing, and the animal usually ends up feeling miserable."

Eadric waggled the crab, and its legs flapped. "What do you want to do with this thing, Emma? I think you should save it for Haywood. You know how much he likes to eat crabs."

The crab's claws stiffened, and it twisted its eyestalks to look at me. "Is Haywood that fuzzy monster that was eating my friends?"

I nodded. "He's an otter, and he likes to eat lots of things."

"Please," said the crab, pulling its little legs in toward its body. "Don't let that monster eat me! Surely I could come in handy someday!"

I hadn't liked watching Haywood eat the other crabs, and I already knew I didn't want him to eat this one, but I couldn't imagine what a crab could possibly do for me.

"I swear you won't regret letting me go!" said the crab, its eyestalks waving wildly above its head.

"Oh, really! And where am I supposed to put you?"

"I heard you talking about visiting a sea witch. You could take me with you."

I sighed. "I'll see what I can do. What's your name?"

"Shelton, which I think is a very good name for a crab. We pick our own names, you know, and I thought about it a long time before I chose it. My brother's name is Crabicus, but I don't like that one nearly as well. One of my sisters has an even funnier name. It's—"

"Here," I said, handing the crab to Eadric. "You hold him while I get the comb."

Eadric's jaw dropped. "Hold him? Why don't I just chuck him out the window and he can go live in the moat? The last thing we need is a crab tagging along."

"Be nice! You're a prince and you're supposed to set an example," I said.

"But he's just a—"

"And yesterday you were just a frog, remember? A frog who had friends who were also frogs. Think of him as a very small subject and you might find being nice a little easier."

Turning my back on Eadric and the crab, I hurried into Grassina's bedchamber and knelt beside her silver chest. Banded with silver straps, it was smaller and newer than the chest that held her clothes. I opened the lid and found the comb resting atop a creamy fabric embroidered with dragons. Shaped like a seashell, the silver comb was embedded with little pink pieces of coral. It was lovely, although it looked very fragile.

With the comb in my hand, I bade farewell to Li'l and joined Eadric by the saltwater bowl. Although I'd sometimes seen schools of miniature fish weaving back and forth through the bowl, the water now appeared empty except for the tiny castle. Perfect in every detail, the castle had two turrets and a few dozen windows, but as far as I could see, it had only one door, which appeared to be less than an inch high.

Ten

Eadric was staring at the bowl with a skeptical look on his face.

"Are you sure you want to go with me?" I asked. "You don't have to, you know. You can stay here until Grassina gets back."

"I'm going," he said. "Although that bowl is awfully small."

"We'll just have to use the comb and see what happens. I'm sure Grassina knows what she's doing."

"Maybe, maybe not," said Eadric. "Look at the way she handled your grandmother, not to mention the flying carpet. Here—if you want to take the crab, you'll have to carry him. I can't stand his chattering." Eadric handed Shelton to me and wiped his fingers on his tunic.

I glanced at the little creature. "I didn't know you were royalty when I met you," the crab said. "It's too bad, too, because I'm sure my family would have wanted to come with us if they'd known. My sisters—"

I shook my head. "No more talking, please. We have important work to do, so you'll have to be quiet."

"If that's what you really want, Your Highness, but I know all sorts of—"

"Starting now!" I said. Waving his eyestalks, Shelton scampered into my loose sleeve, pulling the lace down behind him.

I took a deep breath to calm my nerves, then undid my hair from its plait and separated the sections with my fingers. Before I could change my mind, I pulled the comb through my hair three times, then did the same for Eadric. I tucked the comb into my pouch, reached for Eadric's hand, and dipped my free hand into the salt water. There was a sound in my head like a thousand bubbles popping, and the next thing I knew we were swimming in the salt water, fully clothed.

I could see the outline of the bowl and the room beyond it, but they were enormous and far away. The castle lay below us, bigger than I'd thought it would be, although in every other regard it looked the same. To my amazement, I could breathe underwater and it seemed perfectly natural. Since Eadric looked the way he always did, I assumed that I did as well, so I knew we hadn't grown gills or turned into merpeople.

Enjoying our new ability, we smiled at each other and then turned toward the castle. It was obvious that Eadric had some experience swimming as a human, but I had not, and so I resorted to the strokes I'd used as a frog. It was awkward, as the fabric of my long gown hampered the movement of my legs.

The castle door had looked ordinary from a distance, but upon closer inspection, we found that it was made of a single slab of a smooth, white material, like a fragment of a giant seashell. We knocked, and after a few minutes a strange creature with a soft, sack-shaped body and eight ropelike arms answered the door. When it saw us, it blushed a fiery red and flung one of its arms across the doorway, blocking us from entering.

"What do you want?" said the creature, examining us with two bulging eyes that moved independently of each other.

Flustered by the way it was looking at us, I cleared my throat and said, "We've come to see Coral, the sea witch."

"Well, then, hurry and come inside before you let the cold water in."

The water seemed warm enough to me, but I followed the creature inside with Eadric bumping into me from behind. Once the door was closed, the creature looked us over again as if it wasn't sure it should have let us in.

"Wait here," it said, and floated through a nearby opening, leaving us standing in a narrow hallway.

I was tugging on my hair, gathering it into my hands,

when I realized that someone had entered the hall. Turning my head, I saw Eadric's face first, his expression so foolish that I had a good idea who it was before I even saw her.

"May I help you?" asked a voice melodious enough to make a nightingale sound like a half-strangled dog. When I saw her, I understood Eadric's reaction. She was gorgeous, with silver and dark blue hair even longer than mine, slanted dark blue eyes and pale skin with a faint tinge of green.

"I'm Emma, and this is my friend Eadric," I said, before Eadric could say anything. "My aunt Grassina suggested that we come visit you, if you're Coral, that is."

"I remember you!" said the sea witch. "I saw you in your aunt's room when you were just a little girl. You looked almost as surprised as I felt."

"That was me," I said.

"Come in, come in!" she said, ushering us down the hall. "You're just in time to join us for lunch. I have some friends over today and we were about to start, but there's plenty of room and more food than we could possibly eat."

"I don't know if we have time for—" I began.

Eadric grabbed my arm and pulled me toward him. "Be polite," he whispered in my ear, adding in a louder voice, "That would be wonderful."

We followed Coral through the door, down a short hallway and into a magnificent room. The walls and high ceiling were pink coral, the floor a bed of pure white sand. A table and eight chairs carved from some enormous creature's bones occupied the center of the room. Purple and yellow fanlike decorations had been arranged in a centerpiece around which tiny pink and yellow fish darted.

"These are my friends," Coral said, gesturing to five beautiful mermaids seated around the table. "This is Marina." A young mermaid with violet hair and amethyst eyes smiled in greeting. Another was named Kelpia and had dark green hair pulled back by two living starfish. Sandy had pale blond hair laced with darker strands of gold. She nodded hello to me, then turned and blew a kiss to Eadric. I was watching the color creep up his cheeks, so I almost didn't catch Pearl's name; she was a mermaid with striking silver eyes and pure white hair. At the far end of the table sat Starr, whose scarlet locks made my own hair look washed out. Each sat with her fishlike tail curled under her chair. Each had skin that bore at least a touch of green. Food and a room full of beautiful, green-skinned women. Eadric would certainly like it here!

"My friends and I have been rehearsing all morning," said Coral. "We get together to sing a few times a week. People call us the Sirens."

Eadric's eyes lit up. "I think I've heard of you. Aren't you the ones who sing to passing sailors?"

Starr shook her head and sighed. "Don't believe everything you hear. We never try to lure them onto the rocks. We're not responsible for the things our audience does."

Gliding to the head of the table, our hostess gestured toward two chairs. "Please be seated."

Eadric darted ahead, taking the chair beside Sandy, the blond mermaid, and leaving me the seat next to Coral. I was happy to sit beside my aunt's friend, but I was annoyed with Eadric, who was behaving as if I didn't exist. I bumped his arm to get his attention. When he didn't seem to notice, I decided to ignore him and let him make a fool of himself. I don't know what he said to Sandy, just that she found it terribly funny and burst into dainty peals of laughter that couldn't have been more unlike my laugh. I wondered how he would act toward her if I turned her into a patch of algae.

We hadn't been seated for long when the sacklike creature entered the room bearing four large bowls wrapped in four of its arms. A small parade of lobsters and snails followed. Using its free arms, the sack-creature picked up the first pair of lobsters and snails and dropped them on the table. After the monster had set a bowl on the snail's shell, the lobster climbed aboard. I couldn't imagine what was going on until the snail inched its way to Coral's plate. The mermaid nodded and the lobster dipped its claws into the bowl, serving her a portion of seaweed.

The snails continued their circuit around the table even after everyone had been served, perhaps on the chance that someone might want more. Each of the four serving bowls held some kind of seaweed. I suppose they were different, but they all looked alike to me, and I found myself wishing I'd eaten more bread and cheese when I'd had the chance.

Served raw, the seaweed was chewy, hard to swallow and too salty for me. After the first few bites, I just pushed it around my plate, wishing that a few large dogs sat under the table waiting for scraps the way they did at home.

I'd almost convinced myself to take another bite when Coral leaned toward me and said, "Now tell me, Emma, what is the reason for this delightful visit?"

I set down my fork, grateful for the excuse. "Actually, we're looking for something and hoped that you might be able to help us. We need to find some mother-of-pearl."

Coral smiled. "Is that all? Then you need look no further. I have some very fine specimens here in the castle. Octavius, please bring us one of the shells."

The sack-creature had been waiting in the corner so quietly that I'd forgotten that it was there. When it left the room, its eight arms appeared to ooze bonelessly across the floor, while the one eye that I could see jerked back and forth, looking first in one direction, then another.

"I don't mean to be nosy," I said, turning to Coral, "but how did you get a sea monster to work for you?"

Coral giggled and covered her mouth with her hand. "Octavius isn't a sea monster, he's an octopus! They make the best butlers. I don't know what I'd do without him. He can do more than one job at a time, and he's all the defense I need."

Octavius returned only a few minutes later with a large seashell. Extending his arm, he set it on the table in front of me. I heard a tiny pop as a disc on one of his arms let go of the shell, which looked like a flattened wheat bun sprinkled with sugar. Rubbing my fingers along a row of small holes, I wondered why anyone would think it special.

"Turn it over," urged Kelpia. The shell was rough and coarse, so I was surprised when I flipped it over and found a smooth, lustrous lining of creamy white with pink and blue shimmering highlights.

"Now, that's mother-of-pearl!" said Starr, the mermaid with the scarlet hair.

It was beautiful, but it wasn't at all what I'd expected. I must have let my disappointment show, for Coral asked, "What's wrong?"

"Nothing's wrong," I said. "It's just that I don't see any hair."

A wave of laughter swept through the room. "Why in Neptune's name would you expect to find hair?" giggled Starr.

"It has to have hair. We've come here to get a gossamer hair of mother-of-pearl."

Someone gasped. I looked around and saw the white-haired mermaid cover her mouth with her hand and flee the room, knocking over her chair. The other mermaids looked away, avoiding my eyes as if I'd done something shameful. "What is it?" I asked. "Did I say something wrong?"

Coral shook her head, making her hair swirl around her like a blue halo. "Not really. Pearl's just a little sensitive about her mother. Whoever told you to get a gossamer hair of mother-of-pearl was trying to trick you. There is no hair on mother-of-pearl. However, the mother of Pearl is Nastia Nautica, who has hair so fine it's almost transparent. I suppose you can call it gossamer. Why do you need this hair?"

"It's one of the things we need to turn Grassina's betrothed back into his human self. My grandmother changed him into an otter and—"

Coral clasped her hands in front of her chin and beamed. "You mean Grassina finally found Haywood? But that's wonderful! Of course we'll help you get the hair. I'll talk to Pearl about it. Under the circumstances, I'm sure she'll be glad to take you."

Kelpia cleared her throat and gave Coral a look.

"Maybe *glad* isn't the right word," said Coral, "but Pearl has heard Grassina's story and I'm sure she'll do it. We mermaids have soft spots in our hearts when it comes to true love. You stay here and finish your meal. I'll go talk to her."

I felt awful about upsetting Pearl, but I had no idea how to apologize. "I didn't mean to—"

"You couldn't have known," said Kelpia. "Pearl's mother is a sea witch, and she's a great embarrassment to our sweet Pearl. If you really want that hair, you're going to have to see her yourself." Leaning toward me, she lowered her voice. "Just be careful when you go. Nastia's nickname is Nasty for a reason. Not all sea witches are as nice as Coral."

Eleven

"I 'll take you to see my mother," said Pearl, "but I can't guarantee that she'll help you."

"I understand," I said. "I can't make promises for my mother, either."

"My sisters have already moved to another ocean to get away from her. I'm sorry I overreacted at Coral's, but I couldn't bear hearing my friends talk about Mother. It's just that she's always doing things…. You'll see what I mean when you meet her."

As we swam, I began to envy Pearl's lack of confining clothes. Blue and green scales covered her from the waist down, while shells and some kind of sea foam dressed her upper body. A string of seed pearls woven into her hair kept it under control. Unhampered by trailing fabric or constricting laces, Pearl's movements were so fluid, they appeared effortless. I was fascinated by the way her tail moved up and down and by how quickly it could propel her through the water. My clumsy attempts at swimming were as exhausting as they were slow.

After crossing the bare ocean floor, we entered a kind of forest composed of a great stand of seaweed swaying in the current. Alleyways opened and closed with the movement of the plants, confusing the way.

"We're getting close," Pearl told us after some time. "I'll help you however I can, but you're going to have to do whatever my mother says if you want that hair. Tell her that you've come to ask a favor of her. She'll give you a task to perform. Once you've completed it, you should ask for the hair."

"I'm sure we can handle it," said Eadric, resting his hand on my shoulder. I was still annoyed with him for the way he'd acted in Coral's castle, so I shook off his hand and swam after Pearl, leaving him to follow as best he could.

The seaweed parted, revealing the hulk of a round-bellied ship lying on its side. A gaping hole exposed the heavy planking and allowed us easy access. Pearl led us through the dimly lit interior, stopping here and there to point out handholds that we should avoid or rotten sections of flooring that would crumble if touched. Brightly colored fish darted out of our way, while a long, snakelike creature with a flattened tail wiggled past. What light there was slanted through holes in the hull at strange angles. I tried to picture where we were in the ship.

Entering a short passageway, we reached a large cabin that appeared to be someone's living quarters. My eyes were drawn to an opening in the opposite wall where a wide window must have provided the captain with a wonderful view of the ship's wake. A high-backed chair sat facing the window, angled so that anyone sitting there could watch the creatures swimming by.

"What do you want, Pearl?" asked a voice from the chair, and I realized that someone was in the room with us.

"Some friends of mine have come to see you, Mother," said the mermaid, motioning for us to stay back. "They have a favor to ask."

An old sea witch rose from the chair and floated toward us. Her hair was indeed so fine as to be almost transparent. Her scales, which reached her collarbone, were a dark shade of green. Her nose was thin and pointed; her pale green skin was taut, as if she defied wrinkles to appear. Yet it was her eyes that made me stop and stare. They were terrifying, so dark and lifeless that they seemed to be two black holes.

"A favor?" said the sea witch. "You mean they didn't come here just to gawk?"

"A favor, yes, that's right," I said, embarrassed that I'd been caught staring.

Something inside a sea chest growled. Snatching a long pole from where it leaned against the wall, Nastia

Nautica rapped the chest until the growling stopped. When the sea witch turned to me, I shrank back from those terrible eyes. "Before you can ask a favor, you must earn the right. Bring me the giant pearl that the ancient sea monster guards before the sun sets this day and I will grant your favor. However, if you don't succeed, I will cut off your heads and feed them to the sharks." Raising her arm, the sea witch pointed at a wall where a long-bladed knife rested on two curving hooks. I gulped and backed away.

Pearl's mouth dropped open when she heard her mother's threat, but her amazement quickly turned into anger. "A beheading, Mother? Isn't that a little severe?"

"Not if they want a favor."

"But they're friends of mine. You can't threaten to cut off my friends' heads!"

"I can do whatever I want to, my dear. This is my home, and they came here to ask something of me."

"You're always saying, 'Pearl, why don't you ever introduce me to your friends?' This is why, Mother! This is exactly why I never bring my friends around! I like my friends the way they are—with their heads still attached!"

Eadric took my arm and pulled me to the side. "Maybe we'd better go," he whispered. "We don't want to get in the middle of a family argument."

I nodded. "We can come back later."

"Believe what you want, daughter. Your friends will

have to get that pearl from the sea monster or I'm using my carving knife!"

We fled the cabin without waiting to hear the end of their argument. The moment we were outside the wreck, Eadric turned to me and said, "Emma, we're going home. That sea witch is crazy. No hair is worth losing your head! I'm sure your aunt wouldn't want you to take any unreasonable risks, and I'd call this unreasonable."

Getting the hair was going to be far more dangerous than I'd expected. If Grassina knew what the old sea witch had threatened to do, she would have whisked us away in an instant, but she wasn't there and I couldn't forget the look of fear in my mother's eyes and the worry on my father's face.

"I can't give up now, Eadric. You can go home, but if I don't get that hair, Grassina won't be able to turn Haywood back and she won't be in any condition to help my father. If Greater Greensward goes to war without any magic on its side, East Aridia will win, my father will lose his western land and I'll have to marry Jorge. I am going to get that hair with or without your help!"

"Huh," grunted Eadric. "If you put it that way… We should hurry if we're going to find that pearl before sunset."

Suddenly, someone raced through the gap in the wall. I thought it was Nastia Nautica coming to cut off our heads without giving us a chance, but I was wrong. It was Pearl.

"I wanted to tell you where to find the sea monster. It never occurs to my mother to give directions. The seaweed thins out on this side of the ship. Swim straight ahead until you're in the clear. Follow the first reef you come to. It will look like a ridge made of coral. When you reach a gap in the reef, turn right. Look for the biggest cave and you'll find the sea monster. It's one of the old species that you don't see very often anymore. The Old Wizard of the Sea cast a spell on it so it would guard the pearl until he came back. It's been there for as long as anyone can remember. Do you have all that?"

"Sure," said Eadric, tapping his forehead. "I've got a mind like a wolf trap."

I rolled my eyes. "Thanks for your help, Pearl."

Pearl shrugged. "Any friend of Coral's is a friend of mine. I should keep an eye on Mother and make sure she doesn't pull any of her tricks. See you when you get back."

Twelve

The seaweed thinned after only a few yards. We spotted the reef right away, a great colony of coral that must have been growing for many years. The pinks, greens, yellows and oranges were as beautiful as any flower garden, the branching towers more intricate than any castle ever built. We passed sea fans like those that had decorated Coral's table and fish so brilliantly colored they could rival the most exotic birds. More than once I noticed eyes watching us from niches and tails disappearing into crannies.

The reef curved like the arc of a giant circle, seeming to go on forever, but we finally reached the gap Coral had mentioned. A sunken island lay ahead, its base riddled with caves, its top worn away by the scouring waves. Even from a distance, we could tell which cave was the largest because the others were small nooks in comparison. Jagged rocks guarded both the ceiling and the floor of the wide entrance.

Swimming toward the cave, we searched for some sign of the sea monster. There was nothing that might indicate that a monster lived there, no pile of bones, no scarring of the ocean floor, no ominous growl or glint of hungry eyes. Instead, yellow and turquoise fish darted through the entrance, flashing here and there as they changed direction. I followed Eadric into the cave; the rocks were sharp, snagging my skirt and tearing it. Smaller rocks, equally jagged and dangerous, protruded from the ground beside the larger ones. I tried not to touch the floor, for it looked odd—red, soft and squishy like a strange kind of coral that grew sideways rather than up. The cave was fairly large, nearly twelve feet across, but there was no sign of the pearl. There was a narrow opening at the back of the cave, however, and I had the awful feeling that there was where we'd have to go.

Eadric agreed. "Let me go first," he said. "I've dealt with more monsters than you have."

"What are you talking about? You don't know any more about sea monsters than I do."

"Monsters are monsters, no matter where you find them." Eadric peered into the opening and waved me back. "There's a passage here. You'd better stay behind. It's so dark I can't see a thing."

"Wait a minute. It's too cramped for a witches' light, but I have a candle I can use." Fumbling in my pouch, I took out the candle stub that Grassina had given me. "Let me think about this for a minute. I've never tried to light a candle underwater before."

Since it was such an unusual situation, I was sure I had never read a spell that would fit. I concentrated, picturing what I wanted and trying to think of the words that would get it for me. Eadric had started to fidget by the time I finally said,

> Little candle burning bright,
> Make the day out of the night.
> On the land or in the sea
> Keep your wick aflame for me.

With a muffled hiss, the candle lit itself, although its light wasn't nearly as bright as it would have been on land. "Will this do?" I asked, handing it to Eadric.

"As long as it doesn't go out," he said. "Who knows what we'll find in there?"

I followed Eadric as closely as I could, trying not to bump into him. Being near him made me feel a little safer, although I was still so nervous that I jumped at the slightest thing. When a fish swam past and its tail brushed my cheek, I shrieked and grabbed Eadric's arm, certain that the monster had found us.

"What is it?" Eadric asked, whirling around with his dagger in his hand.

I felt my face grow warm. "Nothing. Never mind. It was just a fish."

"Huh," he grunted, shaking his head. Feeling like a fool who jumps on a chair when she sees a mouse, I resolved to be braver next time, no matter what I saw.

As the passage narrowed even more, Eadric's body blocked most of the light, but I could see that the walls were ridged and kind of squishy. Something wasn't right.

When the passage widened into a small chamber, Eadric paused to look around. "Do you see anything?" I asked as he held the candle high.

"No monster, but I think I see the pearl. That thing is huge!"

"Let me look," I said, trying to see past him.

Caught in a swirl of seaweed on the floor of the chamber, the pearl was enormous. It was almost the same size as my head, yet perfectly round and pure white. Handing me the candle, Eadric bent down and reached for the pearl. When he tried to pick it up, he couldn't budge it. "Something is holding it," he said.

Eadric braced himself to try again and was able to lift the pearl a few inches. "Maybe if I help," I said, wrapping my arms around his waist and adding my strength to his.

The pearl came away from the floor, inch by inch, until whatever had been holding it suddenly let go and we flew backward, hitting the opposite wall with a splat. Slimy globs dripped from the pearl, coating Eadric's hands. When we stood, we saw a depression where the pearl had been attached. Glistening with an oily sheen, a liquid heavier than water bubbled from the depression until it overflowed onto the floor.

I felt a tremor beneath my feet. "Eadric," I said, but he was too engrossed in the pearl to notice. Another tremor, stronger than the first, made Eadric look up in surprise.

"What was that?" demanded a familiar voice. I glanced down and saw the little green crab climbing up from the folds of my hem. "You forgot about me already, didn't you? I know it's because I'm so little. If I were as big as one of my brothers, you'd never forget that I was around. My brother Clawson—"

The next tremor was enough to make me stagger.

"What are you waiting for?" asked the little crab. "Get out of here while you still can! I'm a little dizzy, but it looks to me like those walls are moving in."

"Eadric," I said, "we've got to go!"

He put his hand on the small of my back and propelled me toward the passage. "You go first."

With the little crab tickling my arm as he crawled into my sleeve, I dove toward the opening. We had gone only a few feet when the walls pressed close enough to brush my shoulders, and Eadric had to turn sideways to move at all. My heart was pounding, but I kept going, deter-mined not to panic in front of Eadric.

The walls continued to close in until they were squeezing me. Many years ago, one of the ghosts in the dungeon had died by being buried alive under a collapsed wall, and he had described it to me in horrible detail. I had had nightmares about it for weeks. I felt like I was living one of those nightmares now.

I squirmed, forcing my way between the walls. The pressure would have been tremendous if the walls hadn't been so soft. I dug my fingers into their surface, dragging myself forward while they squeezed the breath out of me. Suddenly I reached the end, popping out of the passage like a seed from a grape. When I turned to help Eadric, his arm and shoulder were already emerging, but the pearl held in the crook of his arm seemed to be in the way. I wrapped my fingers around the pearl and braced my feet against the wall. Tugging as hard as I could, I pulled the pearl free. A moment later, Eadric slipped out.

We were back in the larger cave and all I wanted to do was leave, so I was horrified when I saw that the opening had disappeared. The ceiling was lower, and the jagged rocks now met, blocking our way. I set my feet down but regretted it immediately, since the floor started to writhe and take shape beneath me. It wasn't a floor at all, but a giant pink sluglike creature that rose up and slapped me against the back wall. Stunned, I drifted helplessly.

When I opened my eyes, I saw Eadric wrestling the monster in a dim half-light. I shuddered when something moved across my arm. It was Shelton, brandishing the fish-headed pin that he had pulled from my sleeve. "What is he thinking?" grumbled the crab, waving his eyestalks at Eadric. "You can't fight a sea monster that way!" Pushing away from me, the little crab swam toward the monster while holding the pin with his big front claw. Shouting, "Leave him alone, you ruffian!" he jabbed the pin into the fleshy slug.

The slug retreated momentarily, then reared up once again and slapped Eadric, spinning him around until he slammed into the wall. I flailed my arms, trying to stay out of the monster's way.

"Take this!" yelled Shelton, plunging the pin into the slug again. A moment later, Eadric had his dagger in his hand and was slashing at the flapping, squirming monster.

The candle was lost somewhere in the cave, but the rocks blocking the entrance allowed a small amount of light to enter. I was watching Eadric and Shelton, wishing that I had a weapon as well, when I noticed that the monster always stayed in the front of the cave, making it more vulnerable to attack. It was almost as if it was anchored in place. I studied the monster, following its silhouette to the floor of the cave and gasped. The monster *was* attached to the ground, but that wasn't all. Its soft pink body *became* the ground and led all the way back to … I couldn't believe how blind I'd been. If I hadn't expected to find a sea monster hiding in a cave, I might have realized the truth sooner, but to have gone so long without knowing …

"Eadric," I shouted. "That's not the sea monster. We're *inside* the sea monster. The thing you're fighting is just its tongue!"

"Its tongue?" he shouted, backing away while droplets of the monster's blood formed a haze around his dagger.

"We have to get out of here! The monster is trying to push us back down its throat. It's trying to swallow us! Those rocks must be its teeth."

Shelton paddled furiously toward me, grabbing hold of my shoulder. His wiggling eyestalks tickled my ear. "We're in for it now!" wailed Shelton. "This reminds me of the time—"

"Emma," said Eadric, "please do something about that crab before I forget how nice I'm supposed to be."

"I think we have something else to worry about now," I said.

Although the tongue had retreated under Eadric's assault, its tip was probing the sides of the cavelike mouth. We tried to swim away, but it wouldn't be long before the tongue found us and drove us back.

The monster growled, a deafening sound that hurt my ears and shook me until my bones rattled, but I wasn't going to let it stop me. It was up to me to come up with a spell, whether Eadric liked it or not. I evaded the tongue while I tried to think of the right words. Somehow, knowing what kind of creature we were dealing with made it a little less scary. "All right, monster," I said at last. "Your people-eating days are over."

Teach this monster, let him know,
That he cannot treat us so!
Where his gums are strong and firm,
Make his teeth loose, make them squirm.

Make them loose until they jiggle,
Make them looser till they wiggle.
So we're not killed while in our youth,
Make him lose each great big tooth.

There was a crackling sound, and one by one, the monster's oversized teeth came loose, although the smaller row beside it was untouched. It wasn't dramatic, but it was effective just the same.

"Now you've got it!" shouted the crab. Two more teeth wiggled in the monster's gums, tumbling to the floor of its mouth. As one tooth after another sagged and fell out of his jaw, the sea monster opened his mouth and howled. Propelled by the blast rushing from the monster's throat, we tumbled head over heels out of its mouth and past the coral reef before hitting the ocean floor.

I rolled to a stop yards away from Eadric. Dizzy and shaken, I staggered to my feet and asked him, "Are you all right?"

Eadric rubbed his shoulder and winced. "Uh-huh. How about you? I thought you were too frightened to be of much use in there, but you were actually pretty brave."

"Not brave, just desperate."

Eadric shrugged. "Sometimes there isn't much difference between the two. So how about a kiss? I think we should celebrate."

"Celebrate what?"

"After what we just went through? Being alive, for one; getting the pearl, for another. And what about your second successful spur-of-the-moment spell?"

"I'll feel more like celebrating after we give this to Nastia Nautica and get a hair from her," I said, tapping the pearl. Something tugged at my sleeve, and I looked down to see the little crab swinging from the fabric, his eyestalks crossed and his legs shaking. I dumped the pearl in Eadric's lap. "How are you?" I asked the crab. When I realized that he was still holding the pin like a tiny sword, I took it away and tucked it in my pouch.

"Nothing wrong with me!" Shelton said as I set him more firmly on my shoulder. "I have felt better, though. Why, just the other day I was saying to my brother—"

"Tell us later," Eadric interrupted. "We'd better get moving. That monster could be anywhere. Look!" he said, pointing back the way we had come.

The monster was gone, and I wondered what had happened to it until I noticed a mottled gray shape curled between the sunken island and the coral reef. It had a blunt head, short grasping arms, a tall, curved back fin and a long, pronged tail. Knowing the size of the head gave us a better idea how big the sea monster really was; it was enormous and could easily have wrapped itself around Aunt Grassina's tower.

The creature moaned, a strange wavering sound that left my bones vibrating. Keeping near the ground in the hope that we wouldn't be observed, Eadric and I swam to the coral reef, staying as close to it as we dared. With the water growing dark around us, I knew that dusk was approaching and we would have to hurry if we were to get the pearl to the witch in time.

Skirting the coral reef, we saw menacing shapes with curved fins and pointed faces circling overhead. Eadric swam near me, his dagger in his hand, his eyes moving constantly as he tried to keep watch in every direction.

When we reached the wreck, it was surprisingly quiet, with only the creaking of the timbers and the mysterious thuds and whistles that we always seemed to hear in the ocean. Pearl greeted us at the door while her mother, Nastia Nautica, remained in the high-backed chair facing the wide window in the stern.

"We got it!" Eadric held the pearl so that the last of the light shone on its creamy surface.

"Mother will be pleased," whispered Pearl.

When Nastia Nautica neither turned around nor acknowledged us in any way, I began to wonder what was wrong. Gesturing to Eadric to stay where he was, I swam around the side of the sea witch's chair and peeked at her. She sat slumped in her seat with her head tilted back. Bubbles drifted from her open mouth, and I could see her eyes moving beneath their closed lids. "Is she all right?" I whispered to Pearl.

"She's fine," said Pearl. "I sang her a lullaby and put her to sleep. She'll be furious when she wakes up, but by then you'll be long gone and she won't have any power over you since you've accomplished the task."

Eadric looked appalled. "Why would you want to put your mother to sleep?"

"You should be glad I did. She told me that if you brought the pearl, she was going to have you steal the crown of the Sea Worm King, a ridiculous request since the crown is useless to anyone who isn't a worm. It's so typical of my mother. She's never been able to live up to her end of a bargain without adding other conditions."

Mother used to tell my sisters and me that she'd give us a treat if we picked up our toys. When we did, she'd make us polish her barnacles or brush the sharks' teeth before we saw any treat. It's why my sisters, Clamela and Anemone, left home as soon as they were old enough. I'll probably join them one of these days."

Pearl held out her hand, opening it to reveal a single strand of gossamer hair. "Here, I got the hair for you. I knew that if you asked her for it, she'd never give it to you, even if you met all her demands. You can't trust her at all. It's gotten so bad that everyone considers her the white cod of the family. I'm the only one who will even talk to her anymore."

I tucked the hair in my pouch and was pulling the drawstring closed when I pricked my finger, drawing a bead of blood. It was the pin decorated with the ruby fish. Pearl deserved a gift for all she'd done, so I took it out and handed it to her. "This is for you. Thank you for the hair and for your help. I'm glad we don't have to go on another errand—the last one was bad enough."

"What a lovely pin!" she said, her eyes sparkling.

"I'm afraid it doesn't have any magic."

"Pah! I have enough magic as it is. It will be a relief not to have to worry about what might happen when I'm wearing it."

Eadric was already backing toward the door. "I'm looking forward to going home. Ready, Emma?"

"Aren't you forgetting something?" I asked.

He had both arms wrapped around the pearl, and I think he was hoping that no one would notice. "Oh, yeah," he said, looking sheepish. "Here, Pearl. Please give it to your mother."

Pearl smiled and reached out her hands. "I'll make sure she gets it."

Thirteen

e had worked our way through the seaweed and were swimming side by side when I glanced at Eadric and was surprised to see that he looked worried. "Is something bothering you?" I asked. "We got the pearl there in time and we have the hair now, so everything is fine, isn't it?"

Eadric frowned. "Why did you give away the pin we'd brought for Coral? Now we don't have a gift for her."

"I guess I wasn't thinking," I said. "I know how fairies act when you don't give them a gift they'd been expecting. I hope Coral isn't like that."

"Why does everyone forget about me?" asked the crab, tugging on my sleeve. "If it's because of my size, I'll be molting soon and then I'll be much bigger."

"What about you?" growled Eadric. "We're not giving you a gift, if that's what you're thinking."

"No, no, no! I don't want a gift, although that would be nice. Maybe if you—"

"Shelton!" I could see Coral's castle up ahead, and I didn't want to arrive at her door arguing with a crab.

"I was just going to say that I could *be* a gift for Coral. I like it here, and there wasn't much for me back at your castle, Princess. If you want to say that I'm the gift, I wouldn't mind at all. As soon as I realized that they were weeditarians—"

"Weeditarians?" Eadric asked.

"You know, people who eat only seaweed. As I was saying, since they're weeditarians, they're not about to eat me, so I'm sure I'd be safe here. Much safer than at your castle once that awful otter comes home. So, what do you say? May I be the gift, because it would be the answer to both our problems, don't you think?"

We had almost reached Coral's castle, and I didn't have much time to consider my decision. "If that's what you really want," I said. If the little crab annoyed Coral as much as he did Eadric, she might come to resent my gift ... and me. On the other hand, we didn't have anything else to give her, and Shelton did want to stay.

"Shelton, let me get this straight," said Eadric. "According to your theory, people who eat weeds are weeditarians. What about animals who eat humans? Say, dragons, for instance. Would you call them humanitarians?"

"Maybe," said Shelton, "depending on who it is they eat!"

138

Seeing movement out of the corner of my eye, I turned my head to look. One of the sharp-faced creatures had come to examine us more closely. "Gentlemen," I said. "I think we have company." I darted to the castle door and tried the latch, but it was locked. Eadric turned to face the creature, bracing himself in the sand. While he guarded my back, I banged on the door as loudly as I could, which isn't easy underwater. "Hurry up, Octavius," I yelled. "Please open this door!"

"That's a shark," said Shelton. "Some are nice enough, but others are nasty. See the way he's looking at us? It's all right as long as he looks, but be careful when he comes closer. I've heard some really scary stories about those guys. Remind me to tell you about the one who—"

"Will you please get that crab to be quiet!" Eadric said. He had his dagger back in his fist and was trying to stay between the shark and me.

"Shelton!" I said, shaking my arm to get his attention.

"I got the point!" said the little crab, scrambling into my sleeve.

The shark was closer now, so close that we could see its cold, round eye staring at us. "Shelton," whispered Eadric without turning his head. "Do sharks have any weak spots?"

The little crab poked his eyestalks out of my sleeve. "You're asking me? I thought you wanted me to be quiet!"

"Shelton!" I cried.

"Oh, all right! I've heard that they'll go away if you hit them on the nose with something heavy. Keep in mind I don't know anyone who's actually done it, so it may not even be true. I'm kind of small to try it myself, but you can if you want to."

Eadric grunted. "Thanks for nothing, Shelton. Watch out. It looks like it's coming this way." Eadric pushed me against the door, then stood with his back to me, his feet firmly planted, the dagger clenched in his fist. I held my breath as it came straight at him, veering off at the last second.

"Got any spells in mind?" Eadric said so softly that I could hardly hear him.

"You'll have to give me a minute."

"I don't know if I have a minute to give you."

"Then I'll do the best I can. Here goes."

You don't want us in your belly.
We'll taste bad, like stinging jelly.
Turn around and head straight back.
We would make a lousy snack.

"Is that supposed to make a shark decide that he doesn't want to eat you?" said Shelton from the depths of my sleeve. "Because I think I've heard that some sharks eat jellyfish, although I may be wrong."

"Emma," said Eadric, "he isn't going away."

"Sorry about that. I told you I needed more time."

"Get ready," said Eadric. "Here he comes!"

I was furiously trying to think of a better spell when the door jerked open and a voice snarled, "What, may I ask, are you doing?"

"It's a shark, Octavius, and it's—"

"Oh," he said, and suddenly his arms seemed to be everywhere. He wrapped one around my waist, and another around Eadric, then dragged us both through the opening. A third arm was yanking the door shut as a gaping mouthful of teeth hurtled toward us. Octavius slammed the door an instant before the shark hit it with a resounding bang.

"That was close!" I said, rubbing my head where I had bumped it on the wall.

Eadric helped me to my feet. "Time to go," he said.

Octavius had barred the castle door. Loud thuds told us that the shark was trying to bash its way in.

"Thank you for your help!" I told the octopus as we followed him down the hall.

"It was nothing. I was merely keeping out some of the riffraff. It's a shame I can't keep it all out," he said.

I swam closer to Eadric and whispered in his ear, "Were we just insulted?"

"Lady Coral," said Octavius, leading us into a little sitting room. "They're back."

"Wonderful!" declared the sea witch. "I was beginning to worry."

"*You* were worried?" said Shelton. "You should have been there. If you had seen what I saw, you would have been worried from the start."

Tilting her head to one side, Coral raised an eyebrow. "Who are you?" she asked.

"This is Shelton," I said, not sure how to introduce him. "He's—"

"I'm your present!" said the little crab. "They want to thank you for everything you've done. And I must say that you have a lovely place here. It's certainly prettier than that other sea witch's home, although not nearly as well located."

"Thanks, Shelton," I said, certain that Coral wouldn't want such a chatterbox. "As for your present—"

"He's delightful! Thank you for such a thoughtful gift. Everyone gives me combs and jewels for my hair, but you can only use so many. A nice little crab who can keep me company is a wonderful idea. Octavius isn't much of a conversationalist. We'll get along very well, won't we, Shelton?"

"You bet, Miss Coral. Why, I can tell you some great stories. And I know—"

"We'd better be going," said Eadric. "If you could show us the way?"

"Of course. Octavius will guide you to the door."

Coral took a tiny glass bell from a nearby table and rang it. "Give my love to Grassina, and please come back again to visit. I enjoyed meeting you both. Now, Shelton," she said, setting the little crab on the chair beside her, "tell me all about yourself."

Eadric grinned. "That should take a while."

"Hmph," said Octavius, who was waiting in the doorway. "Please follow me."

"What about the shark?" I asked the octopus.

"It won't bother you. The world beyond the shell door follows its own rules. Whatever happens in the waters around the castle will not affect the waters beyond that door."

Good! I thought. I'd already seen enough big, sharp teeth to last me a lifetime.

The shell door wasn't far from the sitting room, and I could hear the murmur of Coral's and Shelton's voices all the way down the hall. They must have been enjoying each other's company, for the last things I heard before the door shut behind us were the high-pitched giggles of a beautiful sea witch and a funny little crab.

Fourteen

We were standing beside the tank with water pouring from our clothes when we heard Li'l's cheerful voice. "Hi!" she said. "How'd it go?"

"Li'l, where are you?" I asked, trying to find her in the darkened room.

"Can't you see me over here?" The little bat gasped. "Don't tell me that salt water makes you go blind! Because if it does—"

"No, Li'l, it's just dark in here, that's all. Do you mind if we have some light?"

"Well, of course! I keep forgetting that just because it's light enough for me, that doesn't mean—"

"Lights!" I said, flicking my fingers toward the ceiling where the witches' lights bumped together. A rosy glow filled the room, making everything look soft and dreamy.

"So you're back!" said a voice, and I turned to see Grassina emerge from her bedchamber. Her face was pale and she had large, dark circles under eyes red and swollen from crying. "Here, let me help you with those wet clothes." Pointing her finger at us, she muttered a few words. There was a blast of warm air, and our clothes were dry, although my dress suddenly felt a size smaller and Eadric's tunic looked shorter. Maybe Mother had been right when she said that Grassina might find it difficult to concentrate on magic that didn't concern Haywood.

"Thank goodness you're home!" I said. "Are you all right? Have you spoken with my mother?"

Grassina scowled. "She pounced on me the minute I got back. Your mother always has been a worrier. I've already checked out Beltran's wizard, and he won't be a problem. He's Olefat's brother, Olebald, and he's even less competent than his sibling. I can't do anything about him until he crosses our border, so it will have to wait until after I've seen to Haywood."

"Where did you find Haywood?" I asked my aunt.

"I haven't yet," she said as fresh tears trickled down her cheeks. "My mother is wicked! I'll never forgive her as long as I live. She laid false trails, and I'm still trying to find the real one. I came to pick up a few things. I'll be leaving again soon."

"But what about Beltran? Mother says that—"

"I told you, there's nothing to worry about." Grassina sounded impatient. "Your mother jumps at shadows. Right now the only thing that concerns me is taking care of my darling Haywood."

"Is there anything I can do to help?"

"Just tell me what you've gotten so far and what you still need to find."

"It wasn't exactly what we expected, but we got the gossamer hair of mother of Pearl." I opened my pouch and handed the hair to Grassina. "And here's your comb," I said, handing her that as well. "Your friends were very helpful."

"Can they have the fruit tarts now?" said Li'l.

Grassina shrugged. "They can if they're hungry."

"I love those things!" Eadric said, hurrying toward the table where Li'l had just uncovered a platter of tarts. After stuffing a tart in his mouth, he carried the platter to the soft, moss-colored carpet in front of the hearth. I sat down beside him and held my hands toward the warmth of the fire.

Li'l landed on the floor and cocked her head to the side. Peering up at me, she asked, "What else do you need to get?"

"Since we have the hair, we need the breath of a dragon green, a feather from an aged horse, and the husk of a magic bean."

"You don't have to get them in any special order." Grassina wiped her eyes with the back of her hand and settled into one of the chairs. "And I know where you can go next, although you'll have to wait until tomorrow morning. You need your rest, and the magic market is closed now, anyway." She pointed at the tapestry behind me, and I turned around to look.

It was an old tapestry that had hung on the wall since before I was born. The picture showed a town centered around a marketplace; it was fairly dark now, with only a few lights glowing in the windows. When I was younger, I'd spent hours studying it, delighted with the way it changed from one second to the next.

"Not only is that the map of a real place," said Grassina, "it's also the best way to reach the magic market. Just touch the wall surrounding the fountain and you'll go straight there. Touch it again when you want to come home. You should be able to get the magic beans at one of the stalls, and someone might have the feather or the dragon's breath as well."

"Do you think they sell swords at that market?" asked Eadric. "I need to get a new one."

"They probably do," said Grassina. "They sell just about everything there."

I gave my aunt a sketchy account of our trip into the saltwater bowl, leaving out a few details like the sea monster, the shark, and Nastia Nautica's threat to chop off our heads. I'd tell her later, when she didn't have so much else to worry her.

"I want to thank you," Grassina said when I'd

finished my tale. "You don't know how much it means to me that you two are helping." She smiled at us through drying tears. "I couldn't possibly look for Haywood as well as find those things. I don't know what I'd do without you."

"We're glad we can help," I said.

After saying good night, I went downstairs to sleep in my own bed. Tired as I was, I still couldn't fall asleep because I couldn't stop worrying. Without Grassina's help, my father's men would be unprepared to face an opponent armed with magic, yet my aunt wasn't doing a thing about it. If only I hadn't led her to Haywood. If only I hadn't persuaded her to go see Grandmother! I didn't agree with my mother very often, but this time I couldn't help feeling that she was right to worry. Even if Grassina couldn't do anything until Beltran crossed the border, she should be trying to find out what he had planned. When I finally drifted off, my dreams were filled with weaponless soldiers marching into battle against some faceless horror. I didn't stop tossing and turning until I'd heard a rooster crow at one of the neighboring farms.

❧

When I woke later that morning, my stomach was already growling, so I headed to the kitchen for something more substantial than fruit tarts. I saw more soldiers than usual on the way there, including some I'd never seen before. The cooks were busy, but they took the time to tell me that Eadric had come and gone already, having eaten enough for two grown men. He was considered a phenomenon in the kitchen, and the cooks and scullery maids were keeping a running bet on how much he could eat.

I was on my way out, my stomach pleasantly full, when I ran into my mother. "Did you talk to Grassina last night?" she asked. "What did she tell you?"

"She said that she can't do anything until Beltran has crossed the border."

Mother bit her lip and nodded. "That's what she told me, too, but she's wrong, you know. There are so many things she could be doing to get ready. I'd feel much better if only she would make some sort of effort."

"I'm sure she knows what she's doing," I said, although I really didn't believe it.

"I hope you're right. I can't talk to her anymore. She's too distracted to concentrate on anything important and only wants to talk about Haywood. I couldn't dissuade her from leaving again, although I told her that she should stay here and plan her strategy. The woman has lost all sense of responsibility to this kingdom. She was so distraught. If she isn't able to find Haywood or turn him back into a man, I'm afraid she might become melancholy, and then she'll be no use to anyone. That's what happened the first time he disappeared, you know."

I left my mother talking to her ladies-in-waiting and hurried through the crowded halls. Armed soldiers stood guard outside the throne room door, further evidence that my father was preparing for war. Reaching my aunt's rooms, I found Eadric waiting in a chair by the fireplace and Li'l seated on Grassina's worktable beside a small cloth bag.

"Grassina left last night after you went to bed," the little bat said. "She asked me to give you this."

"What is it?" I asked. Peeking inside, I saw a handful of coins.

"It should be enough for the magic beans," said Li'l. "Now you'd better go. You're already getting a late start."

Although the tapestry took up a large part of one wall, the picture of the fountain wasn't very big. Our fingers covered most of it when Eadric and I touched it at the same time. I knew it was woven cloth, but the picture felt as cold and smooth as real stone. A rush of air made me blink; there was a brief sensation of flying, and suddenly we were standing beside a marble fountain.

The fountain was on a small raised platform, giving us a good view of the market. Pausing at the top of the steps, I tried to make sense of the market's layout, but the arrangement of stalls and carts didn't seem to be in any order. "Let's look around," said Eadric, taking the steps two at a time.

A yellow canopy the color of daisies shaded the stall at the bottom of the steps. Pictures of tankards had been worked into the canopy's fabric, and on the shelf running the length of the stall a dozen pewter tankards rested, polished and ready for sale. Eadric stopped a few yards away, his mouth gaping in disbelief. A gray tabby cat with white paws stood behind the counter, polishing a tankard it had taken from a crate.

"Will you look at that!" said Eadric, staring at the cat.

"Close your mouth, Eadric," I said, nudging him with my elbow. "It's not polite to stare."

"But he's a cat—"

"And this is a *magic* marketplace. You can't expect it to be like a normal one."

"Tankards for sale!" sang the cat. "Bottomless tankards for sale here! Never run out of ale again. Fill it once and it stays filled, no matter how much you drink."

"My uncle would like one of those," said Eadric. "Except he'd find it a challenge and try to drink it dry."

"We're not here to buy gifts for people. We're here for the bean, remember?"

"The bean—right. Hey, cat," said Eadric, "do you

know where we can buy a magic bean?"

"No, sorry, mate. I'm new here and don't know the other stalls yet. You might ask the dog two stalls over. He makes deliveries and seems to know his way around. Can I interest you in a tankard?"

"Maybe another time. Thanks, cat."

The pale blue canopy of the next stall showed a picture of a cloud, its cheeks puffed out with lines curling away from its mouth as if it was blowing something.

"What do you have there?" Eadric asked, pointing to a carved wooden box resting on the counter.

A young man with straw-colored hair flipped open the lid and removed four slim pieces of glass dangling from a round silver plate. A silver cylinder hung in the midst of the glass pieces, and as we watched, the man tapped the cylinder. It bumped against the glass strips, setting off a tinkling chime. A breeze sprang up in the stall, ruffling Eadric's hair and the few curls that had sprung loose from my braid.

"You see," said the young man, tapping the cylinder again and setting off a brisker wind. "It's a wind chime, and its operation is simple. Each touch amplifies the effect. Amaze your friends, confound your enemies, command the wind whenever you wish!"

"We have other shopping to do first," I said, seeing from the expression on Eadric's face that he was wavering.

The cat had mentioned a dog at the second stall over,

but the only occupant was an old woman dressed all in blue. "May I help you, young miss?" she asked. "I have some lovely stones for sale." Setting a small chest on the counter, she lifted the lid, displaying an assortment of colored stones. "Stones for every occasion—stones that can make you successful or brave, stones that will cure a stomach ailment or make a toothache go away. These purple stones will banish bad dreams if that's what's troubling you." She held a violet-colored stone in the sunlight.

"It's very nice, I'm sure, but it's not what I'm looking for. Actually, I was told that a dog worked at this stall who might be able to help us. He makes deliveries."

The old woman pursed her lips and shut the lid with a snap. "Oh, you want Archie. He's off on a delivery now, and I don't expect him back anytime soon."

"We're looking for a magic bean. Do *you* know where I could purchase one?"

"A magic bean, you say?" The woman shook her head. "Sorry, I can't help you with that."

A knot formed in the pit of my stomach. Finding the bean might not be as easy as I'd thought.

"Emma, come over here!" called Eadric from a stall on the other side of the narrow alley. A beefy man stood behind the counter holding a stout stick in his hand. Stuffing dribbled from a cloth dummy hanging from a post in the corner. "This stick is amazing! Watch what it can do." Eadric nodded to the man.

"Beat it, stick," said the man, tossing the stick at the dummy. Whirling through the air, the stick beat the cloth body with loud thwacks and puffs of dust. The dummy swung from the pole, twisting and turning with every whack of the merciless stick until I thought its seams couldn't possibly hold together any longer.

"You use it if someone tries to steal from you," explained Eadric. "You never know when you might meet a thief."

I shook my head and started to walk away. "I don't think so. It would be just as easy for the stick to be used against the owner as against a thief. I'll take my chances without the stick, thank you."

Eadric ran after me. "But Emma, you take too many chances. At least with the stick I'd know you were safe."

"I *am* safe," I said, giving Eadric my most dazzling smile. "I have you with me, don't I?"

Eadric appeared to be speechless. He stared at me for a moment, perhaps to see if I was joking, but I didn't let him see how I really felt. I didn't want a stick to protect me; I could protect myself.

"You're right," he said, shrugging. "Let's go find that bean."

We continued between the stalls, pausing to examine the items that interested us, like the acorns that could hold an entire wardrobe and the shoes that could carry a person enormous distances, but we still didn't see the dog or hear anyone hawking fresh vegetables. I was beginning to wonder if we'd ever find the stall when I saw a little dog with white, fluffy fur carrying a leather bag in his mouth.

"Pardon me," I called to the dog. "Are you Archie?"

The little dog stopped abruptly and turned to look at me, the bag gripped tightly between his teeth. He nodded without opening his mouth.

"We were told that you might know where we can find someone who sells magic beans," I said.

Archie tilted his head to one side and looked me up and down. I must have passed his inspection, because he set the bag on the ground, although he was careful to place both front feet on top of it. "Look for the stall with the dark green canopy. Old man Bosely is the only one I know who sells magic beans. If he's not there, ask Milky White. She's learning the trade."

"Who is Milky White?" I asked, but the little dog had already grabbed his bag and trotted off through the crowd, his plumed tail swishing.

I found Eadric nibbling the leg of a roast partridge. He offered me a wing and didn't seem offended when I refused.

"We need to look for a green canopy, a man named Bosely and someone called Milky White," I said.

"It must be another cat. I can't believe what they

have these cats doing. I'll tell you, though, that cat back there really knows how to cook a partridge," he said, smacking his lips.

It took us a while to work our way across the marketplace, as Eadric wanted to stop at every food stall. It wasn't until we'd reached the last row of vendors that we found the right one. A large stall shaded by a canopy of darkest green, it reminded me of the velvet-lined chest where my mother kept her jewels. The colors were more brilliant than those of ordinary vegetables—ruby apples, amethyst plums, topaz squash, and sapphire berries. I saw fruits and vegetables that I had never seen before, like the long yellow fruit that grew in bunches like fingers, and enormous striped melons as big as a horse's head. They seemed to have everything—everything but beans.

A man with a scraggly beard and a shock of white hair watched us approach. He was so short that his chin could have rested on the countertop, yet his hands were enormous and I could see the swell of his muscles under his brown jerkin. The cow standing behind him was entirely white but for the tip of her nose and her enormous dark eyes. I decided that she had to be Milky White.

I was opening my mouth to ask about the bean when Eadric reached for a plum, squeezing it between his thumb and forefinger. The man's eyes were crossed, so it was hard to tell exactly where he was looking, but it was clear that he'd noticed Eadric. "Can I help you?" he said. "We have a policy here—you touch it, you buy it." He pointed to a sign on the table written in glowing script.

You touch it, you buy it.
No free samples. No refunds.
Shoplifters will be persecuted by harpies.

"How many plums would you like?" the man asked. "They're magic plums, so they're guaranteed to be delicious."

"Four," said Eadric.

"What we're really looking for are magic beans," I said.

The man shifted his gaze in my direction. "We don't have any now. They're not in season. Come back in six months. We should have some by then."

"We need them to counteract a spell," said Eadric. "We can't wait six months!"

"Sorry, I can't help you. I traded my last beans for Milky White. That'll be one penny for four plums."

"Is there anyone else who might have some?" I asked. "Maybe Milky White's former owner could spare one."

The cow blinked her long, dark lashes. "Those are

gone, too. Jack told me that his mother threw them out the window when he brought them home."

Bosely grunted and scratched his nose. "As I said, come back in six months. You can buy as many beans as you want then."

Fifteen

nwilling to give up yet, we wandered through the marketplace, asking merchants about magic beans. Most of them looked at us as if we were crazy and said, "Not at this time of year." Others were sneakier, acting as though they might know, then trying to sell us their own merchandise instead.

Although we weren't having any luck finding a bean, we did come across a lot of other tempting magical goods for sale. I was examining a quill pen that never needed dipping when someone screeched, "Emeralda!" from across the marketplace. I cringed, recognizing my grandmother's voice.

"What are you doing here?" she called, elbowing people aside.

"Looking for a gift for Mother," I said. It was as likely an excuse as any, although I doubted my mother would really want anything from a magic marketplace. I had no intention of telling Grandmother about our real errand, however.

Grandmother rubbed the tip of her long nose and squinted. "My cat tells me that you've begun practicing magic. It's about time. Are you any good at it?"

"I can do a few spells," I said. Eadric coughed and I felt my face grow hot, but my grandmother didn't seem to notice.

"Excellent. Keep studying. We need more witches in our family. Come see me when you're ready to learn from an expert!" It was the first time in my life that I'd earned my grandmother's approval, and I wasn't sure what to say. "You haven't seen Olefat, have you?" she asked. "I tracked the old scoundrel here, but he's good at hiding."

I shook my head. "I haven't seen him."

Her gaze darted around the marketplace, settling on a pudgy witch carrying a large woven basket only a few stalls away. "I almost had him in Arabia, but he disguised himself as a dancing girl and hid in the sultan's palace."

"Olefat?" said Eadric, his eyebrow quirked in surprise. "He's an old man!"

"You'd be amazed what a few veils can hide." Squinting, Grandmother stared at the witch and said, "There, on her shoulders. Does that look like birdseed to you?"

The specks on her cloak could have been seeds, although I couldn't really tell from a distance. "Maybe," I began, but Grandmother was already scurrying toward the other stall.

A green feathered head popped above the rim of the pudgy witch's basket. "They're here!" shrilled a distinctive voice as Metoo flapped his wings, making the basket lurch and bounce.

"Not now, you stupid bird!" shouted the witch, struggling to hold on to the basket. Olefat was wearing a disguise so good, I wouldn't have recognized him if I hadn't heard his voice. The hood of his cape covered his head, and he wore a long black dress much like my grandmother's. He'd shaved off his beard and mustache and darkened his skin. When he saw my grandmother jostling her way through the crowd, his eyes went wide and he stepped back a pace, then turned and darted toward the fountain.

"Stop him!" screamed Grandmother. At the sound of her voice, a half dozen furious old witches began to run after Olefat. I recognized them as some of the witches from the retirement community.

Olefat pounded up the steps to the fountain, his heels kicking up his hem, while Metoo squawked and floundered about in the basket. I was surprised to see how fast my grandmother could run once she was free of the crowd. Even so, she was only at the bottom of the steps when Olefat reached out his hand and touched the low wall surrounding the fountain. Grandmother cursed and flung herself at the old wizard as the air shimmered around him. She was too late: he disappeared seconds before her hand slapped the wall. The air shimmered again, then suddenly she was gone as well.

"Why didn't she use magic to catch him?" Eadric asked.

I shrugged, looking up when a merchant standing nearby answered. "Only licensed magic works inside the town limits. The merchants' guild handles the licenses, and they've placed a damper over the town to prevent the use of random magic. Without a damper, unscrupulous customers could steal whatever they wanted and no one could trace them."

Eadric nodded. "Maybe that's why Olefat thought it was safe to come here."

"But won't they end up in the same place?" I asked. "She touched the wall, too."

"They'll go back to wherever they came from," said the merchant. "Can't say where that might be."

We continued on for a few more minutes and had reached the section of the marketplace where potions were sold when we heard shouting. A crowd was running toward us, growing louder and more frantic. Something roared in a voice so loud that the shutters behind me shook. I covered my ringing ears with my hands, while Eadric clapped his hand to his dagger. "I have *got* to get a sword!" he said, his eyes scanning the crowd as he looked for the source of danger.

The crowd opened up, revealing a black-maned lion

and a silver-horned unicorn facing each other. The unicorn screamed, rearing up on his hind legs to crush the lion's skull with his flailing hooves. As the unicorn was about to strike, the lion leaped aside, then turned to slash at his opponent with raking claws. The same people who had been so eager to get away moments before now seemed more interested in gawking.

"We'd better go," I said. "We don't have time to stay and watch."

"I want to see how it ends."

"Fine," I said, starting to walk. "You stay here while I keep looking."

"Can't you wait another minute?"

"Not if we want to look for the bean *and* a sword."

"Oh, right," said Eadric, hurrying after me.

I was almost ready to abandon our search for the bean, when we reached a stall with a faded gray canopy and an assortment of merchandise for sale. A white-haired old woman looked up as we drew near. She smiled toothlessly and said, "What can I do for you?" Even if she'd had teeth, her appearance would have been unusual, since she had only one eye and it never seemed to look directly at us, rolling around in its socket as if it had a life of its own.

"We're looking for magic beans," Eadric said bluntly. "Do you have any?"

"You're out of luck. No beans this time of year.

They're out of season."

"Maybe you can still help us," I said to the old woman. "Do you know anyone who has dragon's breath for sale? Or a horse feather or two?"

"Dragon's breath is rare. It's too hard to collect without getting fried. I've never heard of horse feathers. Are you sure someone isn't playing a trick on you?"

"It's possible, but it isn't likely. We'll just have to keep looking," I said and began to turn away.

"Perhaps I have something else you might like. Let me see." The old woman bent over, reaching under the counter for something, but as she leaned down, her eye popped out, rolled across the counter and fell to the ground with a soft plop.

Eadric bent down to search the ground for the eye. *He's a kind person,* I thought, watching him pick up the filthy eye and hand it to the old witch. A lot of people wouldn't have wanted to touch it.

"Thanks," said the woman. "I used to have a jar of them, but my husband took it when he ran off with a younger witch. When I finally caught up with him, he and his little tart had already broken up and he'd left the eyes with her. I never did find out the name of the witch or what had become of my jar of eyeballs."

"Really?" I said. "I might know where they are."

The old woman gasped as her mouth dropped open, giving off an odor that made my eyes water. "Where are they? Tell me where they are and I'll give you your beans!"

"I thought you said you didn't have any," said Eadric.

"That was before I knew you had something I wanted. I always like to keep a couple on hand. You never know when they might be useful. Tell me, where is my jar of eyeballs?"

"Well, I don't actually know that they're *your* eyeballs," I began.

The old woman waved her hand, dismissing any question of ownership. "That doesn't matter. I'll know them when I see them. Where are they?"

"The beans first," said Eadric.

The witch reached for a box tucked beneath the counter. Hefting it onto the wooden board, she rummaged through it while muttering under her breath. "Magic buckles, magic baubles, magic bones … ah, here they are—magic beans!" Taking two shriveled yellow things from the dirt in the bottom of the box, she held them up between her thumb and forefinger, showing them to Eadric and me. "Now, tell me about my eyeballs."

"Wait a minute," said Eadric. "What are those?"

"Magic beans, of course. They may be old, but they're still potent! If you don't want them, you can wait six months for fresh ones."

"Never mind," he grumbled. "I guess they'll do."

The old woman turned to me. "My eyeballs?" she prompted.

"I saw a jar filled with eyeballs in a witch's cottage about a week ago," I said. Eadric and I had been stuck in the cottage when we were frogs, but I wasn't about to tell her that.

"Were they alive?" the old woman asked, holding her breath.

"Yes, very much so. They kept looking at me."

She clapped her hands, unable to control her glee. "And where is this cottage?"

"In the enchanted woods at the edge of Greater Greensward."

"That's all I need to know! Thanks! Enjoy your beans!" she said dropping them into Eadric's outstretched hand. Grabbing a box from under the counter, the old woman dashed from her stall.

"Now we can go see about your sword," I said, pleased with our newest acquisition. "If we hurry, we can be back at the castle before dinner."

Laughing, Eadric set his hands on my waist and picked me up, spinning me around until I was dizzy. "This day has turned out better than I thought it would! We got your beans, I'm going to get my sword and we'll still be at your castle in time for a hot meal. How about a kiss to celebrate?"

"You and your celebrating! Are you sure we have

time for a kiss? Shouldn't we hurry before all the swords are sold?"

"I hadn't thought of that!" he said, setting me down so fast that my teeth clacked together. "You can give me that kiss later."

"Wait! I just thought that—" But Eadric was already gone, disappearing between the stalls as he rushed to find the armorers' section of the market. I hurried after him, not sure where we should be looking, so I was surprised when I heard someone singing and realized from its words that it was a sword.

> Alas, my master, you do me wrong,
> To cut me off from sight and song.
> For I can serve you oh so well,
> Fighting better and faster than any!

It was still singing when I reached the stall where Eadric stood in line, a look of great longing on his face. There were only two other young men in front of the stall, both dressed in dark green. The man wearing a pointed cap was paying for his sword while the other waited to test one.

After collecting the customer's money, the tradesman gestured to the young man in front of Eadric and handed him a sword. "Here, try this one, young master," he said.

The sword seemed to come alive the moment it left its scabbard, glowing with a soft light that almost vibrated. When the young man stepped to the well-used practice dummy and raised his sword arm, the gleaming metal began to sing.

I am the sharpest sword around.
My blade can cut through butter.
I slice through trees with equal ease,
Carve stone without a mutter.

"No two are exactly alike," the tradesman explained. "They're named swords, the best in the known world. They bond to their owners very quickly."

"I'll take it," said the young man, tossing him a leather sack filled with clinking coins.

The merchant smiled and ducked his head, but he counted the coins before the young man was out of sight. A bell chimed, and I saw other merchants begin to close their stalls, helped by cats, dogs and a few human assistants.

The sword merchant frowned when he saw that Eadric was still waiting. "I'll be closing now, young master," he said as he lowered the first of the shutters that protected his stall.

Eadric placed his hand on the next shutter, preventing the merchant from moving it. "Surely you can take the time to show me one of your fine swords. I need to buy one today if possible."

The merchant glanced at Eadric out of the corner of his eyes. "We're not supposed to transact business after the bell has rung. I'll be back in a fortnight."

"I can't believe that you don't want to sell one more sword. If they're as good as you claim they are, it won't take me long to decide."

"Ah, well, I suppose it couldn't hurt." The merchant reached into a box, pulling out an ornately carved scabbard from which a filigreed grip protruded. "Here's one of my finest." He held up his hand in protest when Eadric began to pull the sword from its scabbard. "No, no! We don't have time for that. The watch will be coming soon, and I must have everything put away. Do you want the sword or not?"

"Without trying it?" asked Eadric. "I'd like to feel the weight of it in my hand."

It was getting dark, and men with tapers were lighting raised lanterns by the fountain. The merchant's eyes flicked toward the light, then back to Eadric. "There isn't time. Never mind, young master," he said, laying his hand on the scabbard as if he were about to reclaim his property. "It was a mistake to think that—"

"I'll take it!" Eadric declared. "Emma, if I could borrow a few coins—"

"Here," I said, handing him the bag Li'l had given

me. "Do you really want to buy a sword without even looking at it?"

Eadric stepped closer and whispered in my ear. "I don't have any choice. When else will I get a magic singing sword? Here you go, my good man," he said, counting out the coins into the merchant's hand.

"I don't know about this," I said as Eadric tucked the scabbard under his arm.

"Let me do the worrying. You've never purchased a sword before."

I laughed and shook my head. "I've never purchased anything without seeing it first, but then I'm not the one who is going to use it!"

Sixteen

When we reached the castle, the first thing I did was ask Li'l about Grassina. She hadn't come back yet, but there wasn't a thing I could do about it except keep looking for the rest of the items. With only one more day left, I was beginning to feel desperate: the two items we still had to acquire seemed the hardest to find. I tried not to think about what would happen if we couldn't find them.

Exhausted, I took my time going downstairs and was surprised by how quiet the castle seemed. Eadric hurried ahead and was already on his way back up with his food before I'd even crossed the kitchen threshold. My mother entered the room while I was looking for a plate. Eyeing my dusty hem, she asked, "Where did you go this time?"

"The magic marketplace," I said without thinking.

"Oh, really?" Her eyes narrowed to glittering slits. "You're practicing magic, aren't you? I knew it was only a matter of time."

I realized my mistake, but it was too late. I'd already said too much. "I've learned a few things," I said, watching her warily.

"I've been telling you for years that you weren't to get involved in magic!" Mother said, her voice getting shrill. "You never can listen, can you? It was for your own good, you know. I was trying to keep you from getting your heart broken. I suppose you're already hoping to be the next Green Witch. Well, it will never happen. You're not smart enough, and you're so clumsy that you'll probably drop the wrong ingredients in your potions. You simply don't have what it takes."

"I've only just started."

"This is a terrible time for you to do this. Our kingdom is at war—because of you, I might add—and Grassina is off to who knows where." Mother sighed. "Your father and I had hoped that the talent would pass you by. The ability to use magic can ruin a woman's life. Is Prince Eadric aware that you're involved in the practice of magic?"

"He knows all about it."

"And is he still serious in his intentions toward you?"

"Yes, Mother, he is. He knew about my interest in magic before he ever mentioned marriage."

"Extraordinary! Few men want to marry a witch, princess or not. I take it that you haven't accepted his offer yet."

"Not yet, no."

"Accept before you do something stupid and scare him off. Men don't wait forever! Now tell me, did you get what Grassina needs?"

"We have two of the things, but we have to find two more."

"Then you'd better get busy. We need her back here concentrating on her work now! Your father has taken his army and started for the border. Our informants tell us that Beltran's army has passed through the Crimson Hills and will reach the border tomorrow night. His wizard rides with him, which is how they made it past the trolls and through the hills so quickly."

"Grassina knows who the wizard is. She doesn't think he'll be a problem."

"To the old Grassina, perhaps, but I'm not sure what she can handle the way she's acting now. Even in the best of times, love and magic don't always mix well, which is something you should remember." Turning abruptly, Mother stalked from the room, leaving me even more worried than before.

I crept up the stairs to join Eadric in Grassina's room, where we sat in front of the fireplace while Li'l peppered us with questions about our excursion. By the time she ran out of questions, I could barely keep my eyes open.

"We'd better get some sleep," Eadric suggested when

I yawned. "We're going to have another busy day tomorrow."

"Before we go, I have to tell you that I spoke with my mother. She said that Father is leading his army to the border. Beltran is only a day's march from there, and Mother is worried that Grassina won't get back in time to help. I just wish there was something that I could do."

"You are doing something—you're helping your aunt so *she* can help your father when she does get back. You can't do everything."

"I can't even seem to do this one job right. We still haven't found the dragon's breath or the feather, and time has almost run out."

"I'm sure we'll find them," he said. Suddenly, I heard the swish of straw brushing against stone, and a figure shrouded in black shot through the window on a broom. Halfway into the room, my grandmother hauled in her broom handle, stopping it in midair. She hopped off with a grunt and turned to look around. Frightened by Grandmother's sudden arrival, Li'l scurried across the table and crouched behind the bouquet of crystalline flowers.

Grandmother scowled at us when she didn't see what she wanted right away. "Where's my old trunk?" she demanded.

"Which old trunk?" I asked, thinking there might be more than one.

"Don't be a ninny!" said Olivene. "The trunk I gave that whelp Grassina."

"It's in the storage room." I pointed at the door and would have opened it for her, but she stomped across the carpet, flung the door open and disappeared inside.

"What's that all about?" Eadric asked.

"I don't know," I said, "but I think I'd better find out." Motioning for Eadric to stay where he was, I followed my grandmother through the door and found her crouched on the floor beside the trunk, clinking the jars together. "What are you looking for?" I asked, trying to see around her hunched shoulders.

"Here it is," she crowed, holding up the bundle of werewolf whiskers. "Best thing for tracking over distances less than fifty miles. Werewolves have an excellent sense of smell. That old charlatan Olefat doesn't stand a chance now!" Climbing to her feet, she slapped the lid shut with a bang. I cringed, not sure what would happen if the jars were to break.

"Now, what about you?" asked my grandmother, leaning close to stare into my eyes. "Have you been practicing your magic?"

I took a step back. "Yes, I have. I think it's improving, too."

"Good!" she barked. "Keep it up. It's the most important thing a girl your age can do." Shoving past me, Grandmother stomped back into the main room. "So where's Grassina, that worthless daughter of mine? I have to set that feeble-brained nitwit straight about a few things."

I shrugged. "I don't know."

"'*I don't know*,'" she said, mocking me in a shrill falsetto. "Well, somebody has to know, and if I don't hear in one minute … Wait, let me guess. She's out looking for that brainless bumpkin Halpert, isn't she? But it won't do her a bit of good. Even if she finds him, I'm not going to turn him back. In fact, I think I'll wait right here, and when she gets home, I'll—"

"You'll do no such thing," said a deep male voice. I shivered as the temperature of the room dropped.

Eadric's face turned pale as he stared at the blue glow taking shape by the door. "Is that a ghost?" he asked, his voice a faint whisper.

"That's my grandfather, King Aldrid," I said. I was surprised to see him outside the dungeon.

"Haven't you plagued these poor children enough, Olivene?" Grandfather asked, looking a little more solid. "I could hear you down in the dungeon. You have no right to be here, pestering Emma and her friends."

"And who's going to make me leave?" Grandmother asked.

"I will, if I must." Although we could still see through him, Grandfather seemed to grow larger and more threatening.

176

"You can't do anything to me, you weak old fool! I have more power in my little toe than you'll ever have, ghost or not!"

"Perhaps," said Grandfather, "but I know more about you than you know about yourself. For as long as you lived in this castle, I kept track of everything you did, even after I died. If you don't leave immediately, I'll tell everyone your secret recipe for witches' brew, the potent kind you use for your most powerful spells."

"You wouldn't dare!" shrieked my grandmother, flinging up her arm as if to ward him off. "Do you know how many years it took me to come up with that formula?"

"Seven, I believe, so you'd better get out of here before I give it all away. Lizard lips and nose of—"

"All right, I'm going! But Grassina will regret the day she turns Harlin back into a human. That girl should have learned to listen to her mother!"

"His name is Haywood," said my grandfather as Grandmother stuck out her hand and snatched her broom from the air when it flew to her.

"It could be Huckleberry for all I care," Grandmother screamed, hopping onto her broom. With a shriek of rage, she shot through the window and was gone.

"Thank you for coming by, Grandfather," I said.

"My pleasure, Emma. If there is any way I can help,

be sure to ask. I'm not stuck in that old dungeon like some of the ghosts. Now go get some rest, my dear. You look like you could fall asleep standing up."

Indeed, my head had scarcely touched my pillow before I was asleep. Even so, I woke earlier than usual and dressed in a hurry, anxious to get on our way. It was Friday, and we had only one day left to find the dragon's breath and the feather.

When I reached Grassina's rooms, Eadric was taking his new sword out of its scabbard for the first time. This sword didn't sound at all like the others.

> Why was I made into a sword?
> Why not a pen for writing?
> I much prefer the written word.
> I do not like the fighting.
>
> Fighting hurts both friends and foes,
> Brings us naught but heartfelt woes.
> If I could, I'd stop it now.
> Never fight again, somehow.

Eadric grimaced. I could only imagine how disappointed he felt on hearing the sword's song. "Whatever you do," he said to me from between gritted teeth, "don't say I told you so."

"I don't really need to, do I?" I said. "It's supposed to

be a named sword. Why don't you ask it for its name?"

Eadric snorted. "Talk to it? It's a sword, not a person!"

"It's an enchanted sword. You could try, at least," I said.

"I will!" said Li'l, hopping up and down. "Sword, tell us your name!"

Light shimmered on the sword's blade, but it remained silent.

"Don't bother, Li'l," I said. "I think Eadric has to do it. The sword has been his since the moment he drew it from its scabbard."

"If it means you'll leave me alone ... Sword, what's your name?"

Light flashed on the blade as it began to sing.

My name is Ferdinand,
But you can call me Ferdy.
I've been told I sing too much,
I am a little wordy.

"My sword's name is *Ferdy*? What kind of name is that for a sword?"

"I think it's a nice name," said Li'l. "It's kind of friendly."

"A sword's name shouldn't be friendly! It should be elegant and powerful, a strong name for a strong weapon!"

Li'l ruffled her wings. "But that's just it. I don't think he wants to be a weapon."

"That's great! I'm about to face dragons with a sword that doesn't want to be a sword."

"Face dragons?" asked Li'l.

"We have to get the dragon's breath, remember?" I said. "Since we can't ask Grassina for suggestions, we have to look in the one place where we know we'll find dragons. We saw one in the enchanted forest when we were frogs, and from the signs they left it looked like there were probably more. Does Grassina have a vial that we could use to collect the dragon's breath? It would help if we could do it while the dragon is asleep, so we're going to need some sleeping potion, too. "

"I might have something you can use. Oh, dear. Grassina isn't going to like this at all." Li'l was still muttering to herself as she fluttered into my aunt's storage room.

"Before we go, we should put the magic beans in the silver chest," I said, holding out my hand to Eadric. "Do you have them with you?"

"Of course," he said, dipping into his belt pouch. "They tasted strange, though."

I couldn't believe my ears. "You ate them?"

"Just the insides. We only need the husk, remember?"

"But they're magic beans. You have no idea what they can do!"

Eadric's face flushed and he looked away. "Actually, I do. They gave me a stomachache right after I ate them, but that went away when the gas started. It's kind of embarrassing to talk about."

"When will you learn that there are some things you can't eat?"

"I'll be fine once I get over this little problem. You worry too much."

"One of us has to, because you don't worry enough!"

Seventeen

$\mathcal{E}$ adric's horse, Bright Country, was happy to carry
us to the enchanted forest. A handsome steed, he
had grace and speed worthy of a prince. His mane and
tail flew like silver banners as we galloped along the dirt
road that led from the castle to the village, turning
toward the ancient trees as soon as we could.

Although it was midmorning when we entered the
forest, it looked like dusk under the leafy canopy. The
trees grew so close together that little sunlight reached
the ground. We had passed through the forest only days
before, but we had been frogs then and largely ignored
by the magic creatures. It was different now, and we
could both feel it. This time, the forest was just as aware
of us as we were of it.

While Bright Country picked his way over tangled
roots, I looked around, half expecting to see the beck-
oning hand of a nymph, the watchful eye of a satyr or
the twinkle of fairy lights. Instead I saw the roots of two

trees hunching above the ground, dragging the trees closer together as their branches bent and made way for each other. The only sound was a prolonged rustle and the creak of shifting limbs.

"Did you see that?" Eadric whispered, his lips so close that his breath tickled my ear.

"The trees really did move, didn't they? Look," I said, pointing to my left. "Those trees are doing it, too."

Two enormous trees lurched across the ground, leaving a space too narrow for a horse to pass. The moving trunks had thick, green-tinged bark, whiplike branches and leaves shaped like the palm of a hand. I couldn't recall ever seeing such trees before. While we watched, other trees began to shift, blocking our way into the forest. I turned to look behind me. The only way still open was a path leading back to the road.

Pulling on the reins, Eadric reached down to pat his horse's neck. "We'd better stop here. I don't think Brighty can take us any farther."

"Yes, I can," said Bright Country. "I'll find a way around—"

"And the trees will move again," interrupted Eadric. "Sorry, Brighty, but you need to go home. It's probably for the best anyway. I have to travel through the forest without attracting attention, and you're too big for that. We're looking for dragons, but they aren't the only beasts that live in this forest. It's even more dangerous here than we thought, so Emma should go, too. Brighty, I want you to take her—"

"What do you mean, take me? I'm going with you, and you can't stop me!" Wiggling out of Eadric's arms, I slid off Bright Country's back and stumbled, landing on my knees. Eadric followed, slipping to the ground with the nimbleness of long practice, while I scrambled to my feet and glared at him. "You need me and my magic to help you get that dragon's breath."

"Emma, I'm not taking you with me. I don't want to see you get hurt. I've been thinking about the dragons, and when I do find one, I don't want you anywhere around. I've fought dragons before, and you haven't. I know how dangerous it is."

"But we're not here to fight dragons!"

"That doesn't mean it won't happen."

"I understand that, but look," I said, reaching into my pouch. "Li'l found this sleeping potion." I shook the small vial of blue liquid that Li'l had given me. "And she gave me a bottle to collect the dragon's breath. You don't have to worry. I'll stay out of the way if there's any fighting involved, but I'm going to do my best to see that you don't have to fight anyone. Killing a dragon isn't going to get us its breath, although magic might. I know my magic isn't perfect, but it's all we've got. I don't want to lose you any more than you want to lose me."

Eadric grinned. "Then how about that kiss you owe me?"

"What kiss? I don't owe you any kiss!"

"Sure you do. We're engaged to be engaged, aren't we? As far as I'm concerned, you always owe me a kiss."

Eadric's lips had barely brushed mine when hot horse breath wuffled my hair. "Should I take her back or not, Your Highness?"

"I guess she's staying with me, Brighty. You'll have to go back to the castle by yourself."

We watched until Bright Country had turned onto the path and passed the more threatening trees. With his head hanging lower than his hocks, the horse was a picture of dejection. "He'll be fine," I said, squeezing Eadric's hand.

Once his horse was out of sight, Eadric and I wriggled between trunks and climbed over roots, running when the trees began to move again. When we finally came to a more natural section of the forest that seemed to be firmly rooted, I relaxed. A flickering shadow made me hurry to catch up with Eadric.

Eadric kept his hand on Ferdy's hilt. I knew that he didn't dare take the sword out of its scabbard until he needed it, as the enchanted weapon would sing and draw more unwanted attention. "Look for a dragon sign," said Eadric. "Scorched bark, leaves brown and curled from intense heat, claw marks ... things like that."

As I looked, I tried to think of possible spells I could say, quick and easy ones that would work against any attacker, but it was hard to concentrate on spells while searching for dragon signs in the near dark. I was studying a suspicious patch on a tree when I heard Eadric say, "What do we have here?" Suddenly, he took two steps forward and jumped into a trench I hadn't even noticed. Nearly ten feet across, the trench appeared to be about three feet deep. "Stay there!" he said, holding up his hand when I gathered my skirts to follow.

I peered into the trench, trying to see what might have created it. Fairly uniform in width, it extended as far as I could see in both directions, but I could find no sign of its origins. "What is it?" I asked.

"I'm not sure, but I think it might be—"

We heard the sound of approaching footsteps at the same time. Even from a distance they made the ground shake. "Giants!" we said in unison, understanding now what had made the trench.

The shaking made the trees shiver and dislodged clods of dirt from the trench's sides, showering Eadric as I reached down to help him out. He grasped my hand and I leaned the other way, falling onto my back when he jumped. Scooping me up, Eadric began to run. I struggled to get down, but he refused to let go.

"You can't run as fast as I can, not dressed in a long skirt," he said, puffing in my ear as he carried me deeper into the forest. I was wearing my old green gown and kirtle, lighter in weight than some I owned, but the fabric was still enough to hamper my legs.

We crouched behind a broad tree trunk and covered our ears. The ground throbbed beneath us, and we had to fight to keep our balance. Peering between the trunks, we saw enormous shadowy figures passing single file through the trench. Although we couldn't see much more than their legs and feet, it was enough to tell us that any one of the giants could have flattened us both without noticing.

We stayed where we were, our muscles cramping, until the last giant finally moved on and the ground stopped shaking. Although my parents' castle was only a few miles away, I'd never known of the presence of so many giants in the enchanted forest. I dreaded to think of what else we might encounter.

A few yards past the giants' trench, I saw a scorched tree. The bark was blackened, as was the ground around it. Eadric found another a short distance away. The burned trunk was still warm; the dragon was probably nearby. We were trying to determine which direction the dragon had gone when we heard a voice screaming for help.

"The dragon's caught someone!" I said.

With his hand on Ferdy's hilt, Eadric dashed between the trees, leaping over downed trunks, while I followed as quickly as I could. The sound of Eadric's footsteps led me on until they stopped suddenly and I heard a muffled oath.

"What is it?" I said, hurrying to catch up.

"Don't come any closer!" shouted Eadric.

I didn't stop entirely, just slowed my pace while I studied the trees ahead. I was surprised to find Eadric suspended in midstride, one arm raised in front of his face.

"What's wrong?" I asked, and then I saw it. An enormous web glistened between two trees, ensnaring anything that tried to pass. Taller than my grandmother's cottage and broader than three of my father's most imposing knights standing with arms outspread, the web was hard to see unless a breeze moved it and the light hit it just right.

A bedraggled raven flapped feebly at the top of the web, its beady eyes fixed on me. "Fly while you still can!" it said in its raspy voice.

Eadric had been caught in the end closest to me, his left arm held in place as if to ward off a blow. Only a few feet away, a flying squirrel hung suspended, its limbs spread wide for flight. Shivering uncontrollably, it made pitiful mewling sounds. The biggest surprise, however, was the creature trapped at the other end of the web. It was a young dragon no bigger than a large dog. A pretty shade of blue, it was covered in overlapping scales and had a raised ridge running from the back of its head to the tip of its long tail. The two wings sprouting between the dragon's shoulder blades beat the air behind it but were too entangled to free the dragon from the web.

"Stay where you are," Eadric told me. With the whisper of metal against metal, he pulled Ferdy from his scabbard. The sword immediately began to sing.

> Why was I made into a sword?
> Why not a—

"Be quiet!" Eadric said, shaking his sword. "We don't need to tell the whole forest where we are."

As if we haven't already, I thought.

Ferdy took the hint. He stopped singing abruptly and began to hum. It was slightly off-key, but at least it wasn't as loud. "Mmm hmm hmm hmmm hmm hmm …"

Reaching back with his humming sword, Eadric swung at the web, easily slicing through the strands. Another stroke and his left arm was free, although tattered bits of spider silk still clung to his sleeve. Eadric stepped back and hacked at the web, freeing the squirrel and the raven before moving on to the little dragon.

The dragon shrieked when it saw him coming with his sword upraised. Puffing up its chest, it opened its mouth and tried to blast Eadric with its flame, but the creature was young and didn't have the strength it would have as an adult. Its feeble trickle of heated smoke dispersed in the air, carried away by a light breeze.

While watching Eadric cut the rest of the web from

around the struggling dragon, I saw movement out of the corner of my eye. I turned my head and gasped. It was a huge black spider, its back as high as my shoulders, its legs longer than a big man's reach.

"Look out!" I screamed as the spider darted forward, its mouthparts clashing.

Eadric whirled around. With an angry shout, he hurled himself at the creature, hacking and stabbing as the spider danced back, avoiding his blade.

"Thief! Scoundrel!" screamed the spider. "Just wait till I catch you! I'll wrap you in silk, bite off your head, then suck the juices from your body!" The spider darted forward, swinging a hairy leg and knocking Eadric to the ground. Grunting, Eadric rolled to his feet with Ferdy aimed and ready.

Humming louder and louder, Ferdy broke into song as Eadric chopped at the living nightmare.

> Take that, you nasty monster.
> Take that, you beastly beast.
> You shall not hurt my master,
> Nor add him to your feast.

The spider had a long reach and greater strength. Keeping its multiple eyes fixed on Eadric, it quivered in anticipation. As if the sword were an extension of his arm, Eadric slashed at the spider, vaulting over one reaching leg, cleaving another in two.

The spider shrieked, staring at the stump of its severed limb. "Forget what I said!" it shrilled. "I'll suck out the juices before I cut off your head! I want you to feel my mandibles piercing your flesh and your life slipping away."

Freed from the web by Eadric's efforts, the little dragon took advantage of the commotion to scurry into the forest, running with the awkward gait of a puppy. I watched it go, which was a mistake, since I should have been watching the battle. Suddenly, the spider was forcing Eadric in my direction.

Eadric had already cut off two of the spider's legs. When he hacked off a third, the spider slowed but kept coming at him with an uneven step. Swept aside by Ferdy, the third leg flew at me like a spear, shuddering into the ground beside me. I shrieked and tried to run, tripping when my feet became tangled in my skirts. Flailing with my arms, I fell headfirst into a patch of puffball mushrooms, crushing them so that dustlike spores rose in a cloud around me.

Taken by surprise, the tickling was more than I could handle. "Ah … ah … ah-choo!" I sneezed, and in an instant, I was a frog again. Too horrified to move, I was still sprawled on the forest floor when Eadric barreled into me. He was a frog, too, of course, but even worse, he no longer had Ferdy.

"What have you done? I've lost Ferdy! I needed that sword to defend us!"

"I couldn't help it!" I wailed. "I didn't sneeze on purpose!"

While the spider looked around in confusion, we hopped under a large fern, hoping that the monster would pass us by. A dry twig snapped. Suddenly, the fern quivered and was gone, yanked out of the ground. "Ah-ha!" said the spider, looming above us, its multiple eyes gleaming with malice. "I thought I saw you go in there!"

"Hop!" shouted Eadric.

We leaped straight ahead, directly under the spider's belly, while its hairy legs skittered around us. A dark blue, foul-smelling fluid dripped from a wound in the spider's underside, and we took an extra second or two to hop around the splashing puddle. The spider staggered as it turned to follow, shrieking high-pitched notes that hurt my eardrums.

"You come back here!" screamed the spider. "You can't get away with this! No one does this to me and lives!"

With all its legs, the spider could easily have overtaken us, but its lopsided gait sent it careening off tree trunks and stumbling over the uneven ground. We hopped around fallen branches, and when our path lay straight before us, we leapted in ground-eating bounds. Eadric was a better hopper and could have left me behind if he'd wanted to, but he stayed by my side, encouraging me when I began to tire.

"I wish I had Ferdy," said Eadric, who wasn't the least bit out of breath. "I was getting used to him. He's a good sword."

"We'll come back … for him … when we change … again."

The spider was persistent, staying on our trail no matter how we dodged and circled. Every few minutes I looked back over my shoulder, hoping I wouldn't see it, but the spider was always there. *If I could make up a spell,* I thought, but all I could come up with were some silly rhymes using *spider* and *beside her,* which I didn't like at all.

When the ground began to shake again and I stumbled and fell, I thought it was just my usual clumsiness, but the ground was still shaking as I got back on my feet. Suddenly, I had an idea. "Head for the giants' trench!" I shouted to Eadric.

"Are you crazy? That's the last place we should go. We don't have any way to defend ourselves."

"That's exactly why we're going there," I said.

The shaking ground had tripped the spider as well. When I glanced back, it was staggering to its feet, keening so loudly it made me cringe. I hurried on, bounding across the forest floor, ignoring the pain in my side and the burning in my lungs. When we finally reached the trench, another group of giants was already in sight, striding along their path. I looked back to make sure that the spider was still following us, but I needn't have bothered. Even the sight of the approaching giants wasn't enough to scare it away.

"Emma, come back," shouted Eadric as I put on a burst of speed and jumped past him, sailing down into the trench.

When Eadric jumped in after me, I didn't know if he wanted to drag me out or if he understood what I was planning to do and wanted to help, but either way it was enough to entice the spider to follow us into the trench. I headed straight toward the approaching giants whose slow, steady pace covered more ground in just a few minutes than it would have taken me hours to hop.

"Emma," shouted Eadric, but I didn't have time to talk. The spider had learned to compensate for its lost limbs and had started to pick up speed.

I was hopping as fast as I could when I realized that with his next step, the first giant would be upon us. "Now!" I shouted to Eadric. Spinning around, I tensed my muscles, then put all my strength into jumping out the other side of the trench. When I soared through the air with my legs extended, it felt almost like flying. I'd misjudged the distance and landed on the edge, my breath whooshing out of me. Using the last of my strength, I pulled myself onto level ground while Eadric sailed past me in a graceful arc.

Looking back at the trench, I saw that the spider was trying to follow us, its remaining legs scrabbling at the soil. With the ground shuddering wildly beneath our feet, Eadric and I fell. The spider, who had climbed halfway up the side of the trench, fared even worse, tumbling down the crumbling dirt to land on its back. In an instant, the giant's foot came down with a loud splat.

Trying to be inconspicuous, Eadric and I stayed where we were until the giants had passed. Once they were gone, we crept to the edge and looked down. The spider was a blotch on the floor of the trench, its legs dark lines embedded in the dirt.

"Whatever made you think of coming here?" Eadric asked.

"I couldn't think of a spell, so I tried to think of how I would kill a spider at home. Stepping on it seemed like the best idea."

"Good thinking, except for one thing—you could have been killed!"

"I guess," I said, shivering at the thought.

"Good going!" said a strange voice. "That spider got just what it deserved."

I looked around, but there wasn't anyone in sight. "Who was that?" I asked.

"I'm Ralf," said the voice, and the little dragon popped his head out from behind a tree trunk, a crumpled violet dangling from his mouth. "I wanted to thank you for helping me. If you hadn't come along, I'd probably be spider food by now."

Eadric smiled. "Glad we could help."

Ralf swallowed the flower, flapped his wings and rose into the air, creating a small gale that whipped the leaves on the trees nearby. Eadric and I had to grab each other's arms and lean into the wind to keep from being blown to the ground.

"I saw you turn into frogs," said Ralf, landing beside us. "That was really something! What else can you change into?"

I coughed and wiped my eyes with the back of my hand. "Nothing. That was it."

"Oh," said Ralf, looking disappointed. Then his eyes brightened as if he'd thought of something else. "You're not werefrogs, are you? I've heard of werewolves, but I've never heard of werefrogs."

"No, we're just having a problem with a spell. I'm Emma, and I'm a witch in training. This is my friend Eadric."

"Pleased to meet you," Ralf said, nodding to us one at a time. "You were both awfully brave. I was really scared when I got caught in that web, but you two weren't frightened at all, even when the spider was chasing you."

"Maybe we didn't look scared, but I was terrified!" I said. "I was hopping as fast as I could and it still didn't feel fast enough."

"Tell me something," said the little dragon. "If you're not were-anything, why are you here? This is a very dangerous place, especially for humans."

"We're looking for a few things," said Eadric. "A green dragon and the feather from an old horse. You haven't seen any green dragons around, have you?"

Ralf frowned. "I don't know any green dragons. How about yellow?"

"It has to be green," I said, shaking my head. "We're trying to reverse a spell. It's very important."

"You should ask my grandfather. He's the king, so he knows all the dragons. I can take you to see him if you'd like."

"He won't want to eat us, will he?" I asked.

"Maybe if you were humans, but dragons don't eat frogs. Anyway, you saved my life and you're my friends now, so he'll want to meet you. Hop on."

"Hop on where?" Eadric said, looking at the dragon as if he was a horse.

Ralf squatted and let his wings droop. "My back. Grandfather lives in a cave at the base of the Purple Mountains. It's a long way from here."

I cringed, mindful of my tender frog skin. "We can't. Your scales are too rough."

"Not at the base of my neck. There's a little gap in my ridge where you'll fit if one of you sits behind the other. It's smooth there and you won't get hurt."

I had never heard of riding a dragon, and after our experience with the magic carpet, I wasn't sure either of us wanted to fly anywhere, but we had only one day left and needed the dragon's breath. "I'll climb on his back if you will," I said to Eadric, pointing at Ralf's wing.

Eadric grasped two knobs where the wing bones met and began to pull himself up. "What about Ferdy? I should go see if he's all right."

I followed, watching to see where he placed his feet. "You're a frog now. You couldn't lift him anyway."

Grunting, Eadric heaved himself onto Ralf's back. "Then we have to look for him after we've seen Ralf's grandfather. You wouldn't mind taking me, would you, Ralf? I left my sword near the spider's web."

"I'd be happy to, Eadric," said Ralf. I grabbed hold of his ridge when the little dragon stiffened his wings and began to flap. Eadric wrapped his arms around me as he whispered into my eardrum, his voice so soft that I could barely hear it over the swish of the dragon's wings. "What do you think of Ralf?"

"I like him."

"So do I," said Eadric, "and I *never* thought I'd meet a dragon that I liked. I just wish we weren't going to meet Ralf's grandfather. We're frogs, and I don't have any way to protect us."

"You heard what Ralf said. Dragons don't eat frogs.

We should be fine. Tell me something. What would you have said if someone had told you a few weeks ago that you soon would be riding on a dragon's back with a princess in your arms?"

I felt Eadric shrug. "I'd have asked her name. A few weeks ago, I was looking for a princess to kiss. I never imagined I'd be lucky enough to find you."

I sighed and settled back against his chest. For a frog who could be all too thickheaded, Eadric could be awfully sweet sometimes.

Eighteen

E ven young dragons like Ralf have powerful wings
that can carry them at great speeds. Although the
Purple Mountains were many miles from the enchanted
forest, it wasn't long before Ralf was following the con-
tours of the foothills and skimming the mountainsides.

Angling into a valley pocked with caves, he suddenly
darted into a larger opening. The cave narrowed at the
back, forming a long, smooth-sided tunnel. It was dark
and gloomy inside, and I couldn't imagine how Ralf
could see well enough to fly. However, the deeper we
went, the better I understood why his grandfather lived
there. Great patches of lichen grew on the walls, glowing
like witches' lights. Delicate crystalline flowers bloomed
on the walls and floors. We passed through larger caves
where columns of multicolored rock rose from the floor
to the ceilings high above. I saw solid rock that looked
like flowing water and clear pools of water that seemed
to be bottomless.

It was cooler than it had been aboveground, but not uncomfortable. We began to smell a pungent odor soon after we entered the first tunnel. The deeper we went, the stronger the smell became, until the air seemed thick with it. The tunnels branched occasionally, and a few of the passages belched hot air. I was happy when Ralf passed those by.

"When we get there," whispered Eadric, "I'll look around in case we have to get out fast. You can't trust dragons, and we may have to escape if the situation turns bad. Whatever you do, don't sneeze."

My fingers were growing numb from clutching Ralf's ridge when we finally entered a chamber larger than any others. "This is Grandpa's treasure room," said the little dragon as he landed on the floor. "He spends most of his time here."

Eadric immediately hopped down while I took my time and looked about from my elevated vantage point. Pink and white striped columns seemed to hold up the ceiling, while squat cones rising from the floor glistened with dripping moisture. All kinds of objects were stacked one on the other in tottering piles. Some, like the enormous mounds of precious stones, were glittering and obviously valuable. I wasn't so sure about others, like the old shoes and stacks of yellowing parchment.

A low-voiced murmur ran through the cave. "You should go over here, although maybe you're more pink than red. Where did I put that other one? I thought I had six of these."

"Grandpa likes to sort his treasures in different ways. Sometimes he does it by size, sometimes by shape or—"

"*Who dares enter my cave?*" boomed a voice so loud that the piles shook and small objects clattered to the floor. What I had thought was a mound of golden treasure wasn't treasure at all. It was an enormous dragon.

"It's me, Grandpa. It's Ralf! I've come to visit you, and I've brought two of my friends."

"Ralfie, my boy! Come over here where I can see you!" said his grandfather.

Wishing I had gotten off sooner, I clung to the ridge on the back of Ralf's neck as he flapped his wings and skimmed over the treasure. My heart thudded wildly; the nearer we got to Ralf's grandfather, the bigger he seemed. The Dragon King was the largest creature I had ever seen. Each of his scales was bigger than a human head and ranged in color from yellow-gold on his throat to red-gold on his tail. The ridge along his back was tall and spiky, although some of the points had broken off and others were missing altogether. His age was evident from the scarring on his scales, the hair sprouting from his long, pointed ears and the way his claws were blunted by wear.

"There you are, my boy!" said the old dragon, crouching down to peer nearsightedly at his grandson.

"But what's that on your back? It's not some kind of parasite, is it? Or have you caught some new disease? Maybe I should find my special ointment."

"No, Grandpa, that's my friend Emma. Eadric is around here, too. They're frogs, Grandpa, and they saved my life!"

I scrunched down as low as I could behind Ralf's ridge while he told his grandfather about the spider and our rescue. The little dragon made us sound wonderful, but I held my breath, hoping he wouldn't mention that we were actually humans.

The king was so close, his breath nearly blew me off Ralf, and the smell was enough to make my eyes water. Blinking, he bowed down until his snout nearly touched my head. He sniffed me, and I could feel his hot breath dry out my skin. When he sat back, he said, "You're right. They *are* frogs. Maybe you and your friends would like to help me. I'm sorting everything by color now. Come see my red treasures. Just don't eat my rose, Ralfie. I know how much you like flowers, but that rose is very special."

The pile of red treasures wasn't large, but it was interesting. A red riding cape lined with a wolf skin had been neatly folded and lay atop a mound of sparkling rubies. A half dozen pairs of dancing shoes shuffled around the pile, while a blooming rose trembled beside a restless magic carpet woven in every imaginable shade of red.

"Very nice, Grandpa," said Ralf. "But Emma and Eadric were wondering if you know of any green dragons."

"Green dragons? Why didn't you say so? Of course I have some green dragons! Would you like to see them?"

"Yes, please," I said, my voice coming out in a little whisper. The old dragon was frightening even when he wasn't trying to be, but if he actually knew a green dragon and could take me to him, our search might already be over.

Turning his enormous bulk, the king of the dragons reached into a mound of emeralds. "Now, where did I put them?" he muttered to himself, scattering the emeralds beneath his groping claws. Squinting, he lowered his head so that his nose was only inches from the pile. "Ah, here they are!" he said, holding up two small dragons carved from jade. "Is this what you wanted?"

"No," I said, my disappointment making the word come out more sharply than I'd intended. "Thank you, but we need to find a *real* green dragon."

The old dragon huffed and dropped the jade figures back onto the pile. "Why didn't you say so? There's no such thing as a real green dragon."

"But they have to be real! You must be mistaken."

"I don't make mistakes, young frog! Kings never do!" I shrank back as the old dragon's nostrils flared and smoke puffed out of his gaping mouth.

"I'm sorry, but we have to find a green dragon to break a spell. Spells don't work if they're impossible to break, and this spell has lasted for years."

"Nevertheless, green dragons don't exist. Dragons are red or blue, yellow or purple, black or silver or gold, but in all my years, I have never heard of a green dragon. Now if you'll excuse me, I was looking for something." The old dragon turned away, his tail knocking over a small mountain of sapphires. "I wonder where I put that scarlet pumpernickel," he muttered.

Ralf sat back on his haunches and watched the old dragon go. "I'm sorry we couldn't help you, Emma."

"It's not your fault. Thanks for trying. It's just that I don't know what we're going to do now. We'll never break the spell if we can't find a green dragon, and if we can't break the spell, the kingdom of Greater Greensward is going to be invaded and I might have to marry that awful Jorge!"

"Don't give up yet," he said. "Why don't you look around while I help my grandpa? We don't have to stay long, but we'll hurt his feelings if we leave too quickly." The little dragon crouched so I could climb off. "Come find me if you need anything."

"I was going to ask if your grandfather had a feather from an old horse, but I don't think we need it anymore. How about some water instead?" I said, rubbing the skin on my back. "Your grandfather's breath dried me out."

"I have something even better," Ralf said. Leaping into the air, he disappeared behind the stacks, returning a minute later. "Try this. It's the salve my mother put on me when I was a baby. Little dragons don't have tough skin until they're a year old. This gunk keeps them from getting fried when they're around other dragons."

Ralf's salve was thick and white and smelled kind of minty, like spearmint leaves. Tilting the vial into my hands, Ralf poured out enough to cover me in a thin, sticky layer. It felt cool to the touch, and when I'd smeared it on my skin, I felt cool all over. "Thanks," I said, wishing that all my problems could be solved so easily.

Once I was alone, I started thinking about Grandmother's spell. If there were no green dragons, they couldn't really be part of the cure. My grandmother must have tricked us back on the island, and I'd been foolish enough to believe her. But she'd been so convincing!

I was wandering around, not really looking at anything in particular, when I saw something move. A group of mirrors, both ordinary and magic, had been stacked against one another. The mirror closest to me showed an overweight peasant kneeling by a fireplace in a cottage with a sagging roof. I was already turning away when I realized that it was Olefat with his hair cut short and his beard just starting to grow back.

"I wonder how close Grandmother is to finding him," I murmured to myself. The image blurred, and when it became clearer I saw Olefat again. He was standing now and appeared to be talking to someone. Although I couldn't hear what he was saying, I could tell from his expression that he was in the midst of an argument.

I was watching Olefat gesture with his arms when I noticed that shadows were filling the room behind him. I gasped when they took shape, recognizing my grandmother and the other witches from the retirement community. The old man turned suddenly, but the witches were too fast for him. My grandmother's hand flashed, and Olefat disappeared. In his place cowered a small, brown dog with sad eyes, floppy ears and a white-rimmed muzzle.

I jumped when Metoo streaked into view, his hooked beak and claws reaching for my grandmother. She gestured again and the bird was gone. A moment later, the little dog began to scratch behind his ear with a frenzied kicking of his hind leg. It seemed she'd turned Metoo into a flea.

Something clattered on the other side of the mirrors, and the image disappeared. Following the sound of clinking metal, I found Ralf stacking gem-studded cups in the gold pile while Eadric ogled a golden helmet. From the way his skin was shining, I could tell Ralf had given him the salve, too.

"Are you ready to go yet?" I asked.

"Sure," said the little dragon. "We can go now if you want. I just have to say goodbye to my grandpa." Setting down the last of the cups, the little dragon left to find the Dragon King.

"Come here," said Eadric. "I want to show you something. Just look at the hinged visor on this helmet. I've never seen anything like it before. I could really use this when we hunt for the green dragon."

"There aren't any green dragons, Eadric. Didn't you hear the Dragon King? And if there aren't any green dragons, then Olivene must not have told the other witches the real cure. Maybe she was holding back her secrets from Olefat. It's all been a waste of time." I kicked a spindle of gold wool lying on the floor and watched it spin in a circle. "We might as well go home and tell Grassina. You don't suppose there's any chance that she'll give up and help my parents now, do you?"

"I don't think so," said Eadric. "From the way she acted before, I think she'd fall to pieces if she thought she couldn't get Haywood back. But I don't think you should give up just yet. The old witches' memories seemed to think it was possible. Wouldn't they know if green dragons were real or not? And just because the king says that there aren't any green dragons doesn't mean that it's true. He's half blind and spends most of his time in a cave. I think we should keep looking. There has to be at least one green dragon somewhere."

Ralf was still talking to his grandfather when we found him. "Thanks, Grandpa. We'll be going now."

"You're welcome, Ralfie. Come back any time." The Dragon King smiled a toothy grin that showed off his fangs. I flinched, and Eadric put his arm around my shoulder in a protective sort of way. The old dragon lowered his head to look at us. Pointing with one gnarled claw, he said, "Those two belong in my green pile. What are they doing over there?"

"They're my friends, Grandpa. They're with me!"

"Then you'd better take them out of here. I'm working on my green pile next."

"You heard the king. Climb aboard, you two." Ralf squatted down and extended his wing. "There's someone I want you to meet."

"Is it another dragon?" Eadric asked, helping me onto the little dragon's back.

"Nope, but he's a friend of my grandpa's. His name is Shirley, and I think he can help you with something. Hold on tight!" said Ralf, spreading his wings. "Here we go!"

A current of hot air buffeted us as we headed up the tunnel. I held onto Ralf's ridge so tightly that my hands hurt. "Where does Shirley live?" I asked the little dragon.

"On the highest peak of the Purple Mountains. He's

a nice old guy, just a little deaf."

I closed my eyes and sighed. If only we could go home now and didn't have to worry about war or magic spells. If only I *knew* that I'd never have to marry Jorge.

Nineteen

When we finally left the tunnel and flew into the open air, Ralf circled above the ground once before starting an upward spiral. "Hold on tight!" he shouted.

The air had been pleasant at ground level, but the higher we flew, the colder it became. Although Ralf generated a lot of heat, keeping us warm, the heat didn't reach his wings and snow began to accumulate, weighing him down and slowing our flight. What had started out as a few drifting flakes became a blizzard, obscuring everything around us.

"We're almost there!" Ralf shouted just as I was beginning to think we might be flying into a white void forever. "Shirley's cave is at the top of the mountain." I was grateful that dragons were famous for their sense of direction.

"Why would anyone want to live on the top of a mountain?" I shouted.

"My grandpa says that Shirley moved here to get away from the flies when he retired. It's too cold up here for them. Here we go!" I nearly fell off when Ralf landed with a thump. "Hold on just a little longer. I'll get us inside where it's warm."

The little dragon caught hold of a string blowing wildly in the wind and pulled with all his might. Peering through the falling snow, I saw that the string led into a tiny hole in the rock face of the mountain. Ralf let go of the string, and a door opened, revealing a hole twice as tall as I was when I was human.

Something moved out of Ralf's way when he shuffled through the opening, but I couldn't see what it was until my eyes adjusted. After the glare of the snow, the cave interior seemed dark, making it difficult to see. Dim light came through holes in the cave walls, and the room finally became visible. We were in a cave about the same size as my bedchamber at home. Its rock floor was level, its ceiling too high to see clearly.

I was startled when an old, sway-backed horse wearing a thick wool blanket whinnied and trotted toward us. White with gray stockings, the horse's splayed hooves clacked against the stone when it stepped into the wind to push the door closed. Once the door was shut, the old horse turned and looked at Ralf. "I know you!" said the horse, nudging Ralf with his nose. "You're old Gargle Snort's grandson. What brought you all the way up here?

Your grandpa's all right, isn't he?"

I bit my lip and tried not to laugh. *Gargle Snort?*

"Grandpa is doing fine," said Ralf, flapping his wings to shake off the snow. "These are my friends Emma and Eadric. They want to ask you a question."

"Your grandpa is dying fast? I'm sorry to hear that. I always liked the old lizard, even if he did have a temper like a ... never mind. You're a young one and shouldn't hear such language. So what brought you all the way up here?"

Ralf glanced at me and rolled his eyes. Then, rising up on his hind legs, he shouted into the horse's ear. "My friends Emma and Eadric want to ask you a question."

"There's no need to shout! So, you brought your friend Amandedric. Another one of those newfangled names? Who's your other friend?"

"You don't understand. One of my friends is Emma, the other is Eadric."

"They each took half the name, huh? Well, that's fine, too."

The little dragon cleared his throat, which was sounding scratchy from yelling. "We're looking for the feather of a horse. Do you have one you could give us?"

"Brother of a Norse? Why would you look here? I was an only child."

"Not Norse, horse! Do you have an old feather that you could give us?"

"Leather? Why would you want my old leather? All

213

I've got are my old saddle and tack, but they wouldn't fit any of you pipsqueaks."

"I didn't mean—" began Ralf.

"I don't understand what's wrong with you young people. First you want one thing, then another. You can't make up your minds, can you? Why, in my day, we knew exactly what we wanted." The old horse yawned, showing us what was left of his yellowed teeth. "I was about to take a nap when I heard you at the door. You wouldn't mind showing yourselves out, would you? My old bones need a lot of rest these days."

"Actually, we were hoping—"

"Don't forget to shut the door behind you," Shirley said, trotting out of the room.

"I'm sorry," Ralf said, turning back to Eadric and me. "I can't seem to make him understand."

"But we don't really need the feather if there aren't any green dragons. We can't reverse the spell if we're missing even one ingredient. Besides, why would we come to Shirley for a feather?" I asked. "I really think we should be getting back." I couldn't figure out what we were doing wasting our time there.

"I thought you knew," said Ralf. "Shirley's great-great-great-great-great-great-great-great-grandfather was Pegasus."

"You mean he has feathered wings under that blanket?" I asked.

"Pretty gray ones."

"Then all we need is one of his feathers!" Eadric said.

Ralf nodded. "If you can get him to give it to you."

"Couldn't we just take one?" asked Eadric. "I doubt he'd miss it."

"Take it without asking?" Ralf sounded shocked at the idea.

"You tried asking, and you saw where that got us."

"That's true," Ralf said, tilting his head to the side as if it helped him think. "Well, maybe we can find a loose one on the floor."

"But what's the point?" I asked.

"We said we weren't going to give up yet, remember? I say we get the feather and then see about the green dragon," said Eadric.

"Fine." I said. "We're here, we may as well."

Ralf carried us to the next room, where he let us off at the door. It was little more than a large stall, with a trough for water, a bucket for grain and a rack for hay. Clean straw covered the stone floor, and the air smelled sweet and fresh.

"How does a horse keep his own stall so clean?" Eadric whispered.

"Magic," answered Ralf. "I've been here with my grandfather a couple of times, and this cave is always like this."

"I could use some magic for Bright Country," said Eadric. "He makes a real mess of his stall."

I peeked through the doorway again. Shirley lay in the middle of the room, stretched out on his side. His eyes were closed, and his deep, even breathing told us that he was asleep. Eadric and I kept our eyes on the old horse as we hopped into the room.

The prickly straw stabbed the bottoms of my feet. Eadric, however, didn't seem to notice the straw and hopped all the way to Shirley's side. The blanket was slack around the horse's belly, so it was easy for Eadric to slip his hand underneath and feel for a loose feather.

I watched him for a moment, then decided that I'd better go help. I was studying the ground, preparing for my next carefully placed step, when I saw something gray partly buried by the gold-colored straw. Stretching out my arm, I pulled out a long, sleek feather. Excited by my find, I whispered, "Eadric!" but he didn't hear me.

I took another step, waving the feather like a flag. Without turning around, Eadric said, "I can't reach his feathers from here," then lifted up the corner of the blanket and slipped underneath. I could see him moving about under the blanket, a frog-sized lump crawling across the horse's side like a mole burrowing in the kitchen garden.

"Eadric," I said, hopping one step closer.

"I can't find any loose ones," he said in a muffled

voice. "I'll just pull out one of these."

"No, Eadric, I found—"

The lump under the blanket jerked, and Shirley snorted, opening his eyes partway. He flicked his tail, whipping his hindquarters and narrowly missing the lump that was Eadric. Lifting his head, Shirley looked blearily about. When he didn't see anything, he muttered, "Darn flies," then dropped his head and went back to sleep. The lump moved again, and I held my breath until Eadric tumbled out from under the blanket.

Wearing an enormous grin, he hopped toward me, holding the feather high. He stopped when he saw my feather. His grin disappeared.

"Great," I said, wishing I could put the grin back on his face. "We'll keep my feather in case we ever need another one."

When we finally set out, sitting on the feathers so we wouldn't lose them, the wind was blowing just as fiercely as before. The snowfall was so heavy that I couldn't see the back of Ralf's head. Comfortable from the dragon's body heat, I closed my eyes and let myself relax against Eadric. I was almost asleep when he shouted to Ralf, "How did the grandson of Pegasus get a name like *Shirley?*"

"It's a nickname, really," said Ralf. "Even when he was too young to fly, he was so surefooted that he could go just about anywhere. The name stuck, and—"

I sat up a little straighter. "You mean he's called *Surely*, S-U-R-E-L-Y?"

"Of course. What did you think I said?"

"You don't want to know." I chuckled and closed my eyes again.

"What about your name, Ralf?" said Eadric. "How did you get a name like that if your grandfather is called Gargle Snort?"

"I still have my baby name, even though I haven't been a baby for a couple of years now. I'll get to choose my real name when I grow up. I want a strong name like my hero Flash Red-Snout. My mother's name is Flame Snorter, but everybody calls her Snorty. She's known for how far she can belch flames. My father is Grumble Belly because his belly grumbles before he breathes fire. I haven't decided on my name yet."

"If I had to choose my own name, I think I'd want it to have something to do with bravery," said Eadric. "Yours could be about your magic, Emma."

"Are you kidding? I'd probably be called Fumble Fingers or Clumsy Toes. Even if it were about my magic, it probably wouldn't be very complimentary. My magic still needs a lot of work."

"I'm sorry I couldn't find a green dragon for you," said Ralf. "I owe you for saving my life."

I patted the dragon's shoulder. "Don't worry. You did your best, and that's all anyone can ask."

Ralf turned his head and peered at me with one eye. "What did you need from the green dragon, anyway?"

"Nothing much," I said. "Just some breath."

"I have an idea. How would you like to come with me to the Dragon Olympics?" asked Ralf. "My mother is entered in the distance flame-belching contest tonight."

I scratched my head with my toe. "Distance flame-belching? We appreciate the offer, but it doesn't sound like the kind of place that would be safe for frogs. Frog skin is kind of tender, and those flames—"

"Don't worry. The salve I gave you in my grandpa's cave will protect you."

"That's a great offer, but—" said Eadric.

Ralf looked so eager. "All the dragons will be at the Olympics. If any green dragons exist, they'll be there."

"But your grandfather said—" I began.

"It's worth a try, isn't it?" asked Ralf.

He was right. If there was even the smallest chance that we might be able to get the last ingredient, then we'd have to go. It was already Friday afternoon, and we had to have everything before dawn the next day. "Of course we'll go with you," I said. "Won't we, Eadric?"

Eadric nodded, although his mouth was set in a thin line and his eyes looked uneasy. "Thanks for inviting us, Ralf," he said.

Twenty

G rassina had told me about the ancient Greeks and their fondness for athletic contests, but I couldn't imagine how the dragons would compete. I wondered if all their contests involved fire.

After flying back down the side of the mountain, Ralf carried us into the same main tunnel where we'd met his grandfather, then turned into the first branching tunnel we encountered. Hot air met us like an invisible wall, but the ointment kept us from feeling much more than a slight change in temperature. It was dark inside, perhaps too hot for the fungus that illuminated the other caves.

Flying through a network of connecting tunnels, we entered a cave filled with bats and another that reeked so badly it gave me a headache. Eadric said that it smelled like trolls, so I was glad we weren't on foot. When we finally emerged from the last tunnel, we found ourselves in an enormous, bowl-shaped arena open to the sky.

With a level floor and high rock walls, it was the perfect spot for a gathering of dragons. It was hotter than inside the tunnel, and I could see why when Ralf flew up onto a small ledge so we could look around. A bubbling pool of red liquid seethed in the center of the arena, the air above it wavering in the rising heat.

"What is that?" I asked Ralf.

The little dragon glanced at the scarlet pool. "That's lava—liquid rock. My dad likes to swim in it."

"Eadric, did you hear that?" I asked, but he wasn't paying attention. His face had turned a paler green, and his eyes looked like they were about to jump out of his head. I followed his gaze back to the floor and understood why. There must have been at least ten times the number of dragons than there are people in my father's castle, with more dragons arriving all the time.

I studied the dragons, hoping to see a green one, but none of their colors was even close. This seemed to reinforce what the Dragon King had told us, yet I couldn't stop hoping that Eadric was right, that the old dragon really didn't know everything, and that a rare green dragon might still show up.

At first, I thought the dragons were just milling about, but as I watched, I noticed a purpose to their movements. While a few dragons darted across the floor on errands of their own, most were heading toward the low stone walls that defined the fields of competition.

Only a short distance from where we sat, athletes raced around an oval with other dragons standing by, watching. A roar went up when a yellow dragon passed a blue one, a sound that would have been terrifying if I'd heard it anywhere else.

A little farther away, dragons wearing armbands ran back and forth between brightly colored tents. Each tent was big enough to fit at least twenty grown dragons, although I never saw more than a few enter at once. I couldn't read the symbols on their banners, so I had no idea what they stood for, but when I saw an injured dragon carried into one tent, I assumed that it housed a healer.

I grabbed hold of Ralf's ridge when a gust of heated air almost knocked me off his back. Looking up, I saw six dragons chasing one another around the giant bowl, flying faster than any bird ever could. A pink cloud floated above the flying dragons, distorting my view of the mountains surrounding the arena, making them seem closer, then farther away. I turned to watch the dragons in the oval ring again. When one of the racers flamed, a small pink cloud formed in the air above him. The smell of boiled cabbage drifted by, reminding me of the magic miasma.

"Ralf," I said, "does anyone use this arena when the Olympics aren't going on?"

"Sure. Lots of dragons come here to practice. My

mother comes here almost every day. It's one of the reasons we live where we do."

I heard shouting and glanced down at the crowd directly below us. A group of giants had arrived, carrying baskets filled with skinny brown pods and long purple peppers. The dragons seemed eager to get at the baskets, following the giants to a low ledge carved into the far wall. When the giants emptied the contents onto the ledge, the dragons lined up behind them and helped themselves to the food.

"Those are flamers," said Ralf, pointing to the eating dragons. "They're stoking themselves with gunga beans and hot flami-peppers. Those peppers are one of the reasons the Olympics are held here. Gunga beans will grow just about anywhere, but flami-peppers grow only in volcanic ash."

"Why do the flamers like them so much?"

"If you combine big batches of them and mix them with a dragon's digestive juices, you get the best flames in the world. My mother eats them all the time. The beans are okay, but the peppers are too bitter for me. Look, there's my mother. Let's go down so I can introduce you."

Taking a step forward, Ralf dropped off the ledge and glided across the arena above the heads of the walking dragons. There were more giants here now, and Ralf had to swerve around them while trying to keep his mother in sight. The giants were sweating profusely, the huge drops that beaded their faces dripping onto the ground and anyone unfortunate enough to be standing nearby. Neither the dragons nor the giants seemed to mind, although some of the drops were as big across as my father's shield.

"What color are your mother's scales?" I asked Ralf as we approached the group of flamers.

"Red. My father's scales are blue like mine, although his are a lot darker. I hope mine get dark like his when I'm older."

"Hey, Ralfie!" called a voice from behind us. An enormous blue-black dragon only a little smaller than the Dragon King was trotting toward us from the direction of the lava pool. His head was huge, his eyes deep-set and shadowed by jutting ridges. When he opened his mouth to talk, I saw a long forked tongue and teeth so brilliantly white, they didn't seem real.

"Hi, Papa!" said the little dragon. With a bounce in his step, Ralf bounded across the rock floor to the larger dragon's side. "Where's Mama? I thought I saw her."

"She had to get ready. The competition is starting soon and she was afraid you weren't going to make it in time, so she asked me to find you. Are these friends of yours?" When the dragon leaned down to get a better look at us, Eadric dug his fingers into my arms.

"They sure are," Ralf said, a hint of pride in his

voice. "The little one in the front is Emma. The bigger one in the back is Eadric. Don't worry. They don't bite."

Ralf's father snorted. "That's good! I don't think I want to know a biting frog."

When Grumble Belly picked up his son and set him on his shoulders, Eadric and I clung to Ralf's ridge, wobbling back and forth until we were dizzy. Pushing his way through the crowd, the big dragon headed to the area set up for the distance flame-belching contest. The next contestant, a large yellow dragon, was lumbering up to the line when we arrived. Nodding to a black dragon wearing an armband, he took a few deep breaths and belched a flame half as long as the field.

"Huh," said Ralf's father. "Not bad."

A murmur went up from the crowd when the next athlete came forward. A slender dragon with red scales verging on magenta, she looked very feminine, with a refined head and delicate features.

"That's my mother!" Ralf said.

Eadric ducked, knocking his head against mine when Ralf's father reached up and patted his son on the back. "Hold still, Ralf. You don't want to distract her."

When his mother began her series of deep breaths, Ralf's wings stiffened, and I could feel his muscles tense beneath us. "Here we go," his father whispered. "Come on, Snorty, you can do it!"

Taking one last breath, Ralf's mother opened her

mouth and raised her wings, sweeping them back as a flame nearly as long as the field shot from between her gaping jaws. The flame was hot, glowing white where it left her mouth, fading through yellow and orange to red where its tip licked the rocky ground.

The crowd cheered wildly as the black dragon raced to the end of the field before Snorty's flame died down. The noise drowned out the announcement of her distance, but it was obvious that she had won. "Next year they're going to have to lengthen the field just for her, aren't they?" an older dragon with rust-red scales bellowed to Ralf's father.

"Sure looks that way," the huge blue dragon agreed.

"No knight would stand a chance against her," Eadric whispered into my eardrum.

It was impossible to get through the crowd, so we waited for his mother at the side of the field. She disappeared behind some of the bigger dragons, then suddenly she was beside us, reaching for Ralf.

"I knew you could do it!" Ralf shouted, flinging himself at her.

"Ralfie!" she said, sitting back on her haunches as she caught him. "How did you like it?"

"You were super, Mama! You're the best!"

His mother laughed and fondled the ridge atop his head. Turning toward the larger dragon, she smiled. "And what about you, Grumblekins?"

"You were great, Hot Lips," the big dragon said.

Eadric snorted, and I poked him in the stomach with my elbow. Laughing at your hosts is not a good idea, especially when they're dragons.

"Guys," Ralf said, covering his eyes with his wing. "Do you have to do that now? You're embarrassing me."

His mother laughed again and looked down at Ralf, noticing us for the first time. "You must be the frogs who are searching for a green dragon. My father told me about you. Any luck yet?"

Eadric shook his head. "Not so far."

"Why don't you three go look around?" she suggested, gesturing with her wingtip to encompass the entire arena. "It will be a while before they announce who won. Perhaps you'll get lucky and find your green dragon."

"That sounds like fun!" Ralf said, squirming out of his mother's grasp. "Roar for me when the ceremony's going to start."

Leaving his parents behind, Ralf flew across the arena, looking for a place to land. While the little dragon studied the crowded fields, Eadric whispered into my eardrum, "What did you think of his parents?"

"They're nice," I whispered back, "but I don't think they take us very seriously."

Eadric glanced at a passing deep purple dragon. Long and lean, the dragon had a surly expression on his face and wary eyes that probably didn't miss much. "I don't mind," said Eadric. "In fact, I think it's better this way. I'd rather be ignored as a frog than eaten as a human."

Twenty-one

There was so much to watch, we didn't know where to look first. Teams of seven dragons each were performing synchronized flying routines in the air above us. The group directly overhead did barrel rolls and flips, then climbed through the air in a giant spiral. On the way down, they went into flat spins and linked claws to form a star.

I never would have thought that watching dragons compete would be so much fun. The giants seemed to be enjoying themselves, too, laughing and talking across the heads of the dragons. I saw a red-bearded giant taking bets, jotting down figures on a piece of bark that had probably covered an entire tree.

Neither Eadric nor I had stopped looking for a green dragon. I saw a gold dragon, whose scales took on a greenish tinge when the light hit him right, but Eadric and I agreed that the color wasn't green enough and that he probably just needed a good polishing. We continued to look, but it had already come to seem like a hopeless quest. In a way, I thought it was just as well. I was a frog now and no longer had the bottle Li'l had given me. Even if I did find a green dragon, I doubted that any dragon would wait for me to find a container.

A squat blue dragon was strolling along a low stone wall that separated the fans from the athletes, urging everyone to stay well back. "Overheated dragons snort fire to cool off," he warned.

"What do they do in this event?" I asked Ralf.

"They run around the arena twice. Then they swim the length of the pool and fly around twice. Most of them end up at the flame-belching field afterward, letting off the heat they built up, but some of them can't wait that long and do it during the race." The little dragon had started to wiggle again, more violently than before. "I've got to go take care of something. You wait here and I'll be back in a few minutes."

"But Ralf," I said as he plucked us off with his claws and set us on the ground. Ralf ignored me. Turning tail, he flapped his wings and took off, heading toward the flame-belching field.

Eadric and I waited by the track, watching the dragons run past. When the first dragons left the pool and took to the air, we decided that we'd given Ralf more than enough time.

"So much for a few minutes," Eadric grumbled,

peering into the forest of scaly legs.

"Maybe he got lost."

"Maybe he found something better to do than spend time with two frogs."

"Ralf wouldn't desert us, Eadric. He's our friend. Something must have happened. I think we'd better go look for him."

"Where do you propose we start?" he asked.

"That way." I pointed in the direction Ralf had gone.

"Fine," said Eadric. "Then follow me and stay close while I try to keep us from getting squashed."

Eadric wasn't always right, but I was learning to trust his judgment in certain matters. He'd lived as a frog longer than I and had learned all the tricks he'd needed to survive. If anyone could get us through a stomping herd of dragons, it was Eadric.

We hopped alongside the stone wall until it turned one way and we had to go the other. Venturing out into the open for the first time, I took my cue from Eadric, hopping when he did, waiting when he waited. We were approaching the first tent when a giant came along, weighed down with an armload of tent stakes. Stopping to adjust the load, he dropped one and it landed with a crash only a few yards away, sending up a swirling cloud of ash. It made a few dragons cough, but its effect on me was much worse. It made me sneeze.

Suddenly we were humans again in a place where

humans were definitely not welcome. I froze, certain that we were more likely to be seen if we moved, but Eadric had other ideas. "I was afraid this would happen!" he said, grabbing my arm and yanking me toward the cluster of tents. "Come on! We've got to get out of here before—"

"Humans!" roared a short, fat dragon with dingy yellow scales and droopy ears.

"—a dragon sees us," Eadric finished, tightening his grip on my arm.

Although the yellow dragon had spotted us, he seemed to be the only one who had. The rest were looking around in confusion, which gave Eadric and me the chance to dart behind the giant's stake. It didn't help that we were no longer covered with Ralf's salve and that sweat was pouring off us. The heat demanded our attention and sapped our strength. Each step was an effort at a time when speed was our only ally, but even speed would not have been enough. No human can outrun a dragon. If we didn't want to be flame-broiled, our only chance was to hide.

The giant who had dropped the tent stake was still standing in the same spot, reaching for the piece of wood. He didn't notice Eadric drag me behind his hand as it closed around the stake. We were much bigger than we'd been as frogs, but we were still small when compared to most dragons and tiny compared to the giant, who could have held us easily in his hand.

I was so frightened, I couldn't get my feet to move, so Eadric had to pull me behind the stack of giants' baskets to hide us from dragon eyes. We used an old folded tent for cover when we heard the voices of the dragons grow louder. Rounding the mound of fabric, we found ourselves only a short distance from the standing tents.

We heard voices inside the first tent and had to pass it by. The next tent was also occupied, but the third tent appeared abandoned. Eadric and I slipped under the flap that covered the doorway and looked around. A low stone bench had been set up at one end. Crudely made, it looked strong enough to hold anyone, even the Dragon King. Someone had dumped a pile of robes in a corner of the tent, although I couldn't imagine why dragons would need them. Aside from a scattering of flower petals on the floor and lanterns hanging from the tent posts, the rest of the tent was empty.

Satisfied that we were alone, Eadric wiped the sweat from his eyes. "I know it wasn't your fault that you sneezed, but can't you sneeze again and turn us back? We're cooked meat if those dragons find us, and they're not going to stop looking until they do."

"I can't sneeze on command any more than you can. Something has to *make* me sneeze." Afraid that I'd lose my nose or do something else just as awful, I wouldn't even consider making up a sneeze-inducing spell.

A muffled moan came from the pile of robes. Eadric

and I jerked our heads around, but we didn't see anyone there. I started across the floor of the tent, moving as quietly as I could. When I heard the sound again, it was more of a whimper than a moan. Grasping his dagger with one hand, Eadric reached the pile first, tossing the top robe aside. Ralf lay curled up in a ball with his eyes shut, his scales a sickly blue.

"Ralf!" I said. "Are you all right?"

"I don't feel so good."

"You don't look so good, either," said Eadric. "You're turning a funny color."

"When did you start feeling sick?" I asked the little dragon.

"After I ate the bouquet Mama got when she won."

I didn't like the way his scales were taking on a yellowish tinge and his lips were starting to swell. "Then here's what we're going to do—"

"Get away from our son!" a voice growled behind me. I glanced back and saw Ralf's parents pushing through the entrance to the tent.

"Dad, is that you?" Ralf asked. "I don't feel so good."

"What have you done to him?" Snorty demanded, her eyes flaring red as she hurried to Ralf's side.

I tried to swallow, but my mouth was dry and my throat felt tight. Even if I could get the words out, I wasn't sure how to explain what had happened before the dragons roasted me.

Eadric brushed past, shielding me from the dragons with his body. "Don't worry, I'll protect you," he whispered.

Grumble Belly snarled and lowered his head, his eyes narrowed. Smoke trickled from his nostrils, and the smell of boiled cabbage grew stronger. I gulped when I saw his muscles bunch beneath his scales. The huge dragon was preparing to charge. "You filthy humans won't get away with this," he growled. "I've always known that humans weren't to be trusted. You kill innocent dragons sleeping in their caves, steal their treasures and attack them when they're providing for their families, but I didn't know you were so low that you'd deliberately hurt children. When I get through with you, there won't be enough ashes to—"

"Dad, it wasn't them. I ate Mama's bouquet and now I feel sick."

The blue-black dragon's head whipped around to look down at where his little son rested. "You mean the humans didn't hurt you?"

"Of course not. That's Emma and Eadric. They're having problems with a spell."

"Grumblekins, look at him," whispered Snorty. "He's turning yellow."

I peered around Eadric and caught a glimpse of Ralf. The little dragon's scales were pale yellow, and the tip of his nose had turned gray.

"Find those humans!" shouted a gruff dragon voice

from somewhere outside. "Wipe them out before they multiply! The things are worse than rats!"

"What's going on in here?" said the Dragon King as he thrust his head past the flap and trotted into the tent. "Good, you caught the humans. Have you found out how they got here?"

Snorty raised one brow ridge. "Through the entrance, I imagine. Ralfie says they're his frie—"

"Would you look at that!" interrupted her father. "A green dragon. So they do exist. Those two frogs weren't crazy after all."

"Dad," said Snorty, "that's Ralf, your grandson. He's sick."

I peeked around Eadric again. Ralf's scales had turned pale green, his swollen lips a deep emerald.

A voice shouted so loudly that it must have come from right outside the tent. "You go that way, Thunder Gut, and I'll go this way. They've got to be around here somewhere."

"Wait till I get my claws on them," growled another voice. "They killed my parents when I was just an egg. Humans don't deserve to live!"

I shrank away from the side of the tent as if they might see me somehow. The ground shook as they ran past, and ash puffed through a small tear in the bottom.

"Ooh," moaned Ralf. "I feel awful." His scales were deepening into emerald.

"Nice shade of green," said the Dragon King.

Ralf opened one eye and peeked up at his father. "Am I really green?"

Grumble Belly nodded. "But I'm sure it's only a temporary condition," he said in an overly hearty voice. "You'll be back to blue in no time."

"I need to breathe into something," said Ralf, trying to raise his head.

"What's wrong, sweetie? Are you having trouble breathing?" asked his mother. Ralf moaned again, and his mother turned to her mate. "Grumblekins, we have to find the healer. This is serious."

"No, Mama," Ralf whispered. "I need to do it for Emma."

Suddenly, I understood. Despite his illness, Ralf was thinking of Eadric and me and our quest for dragon's breath. If he did what he proposed, we'd have everything we were looking for, but even so …

"That's all right, Ralf. You don't have to do that. You just have to get well, and I think I know how to help you."

Ralf shook his head. "Not until I help you first. Do you have something?"

I shoved my hand into my pouch and grabbed the bottle. Yanking out the stopper, I knelt beside Ralf and held the bottle to his nose. He puffed a few gasping breaths, filling the small container, then lay back, his eyes half closed.

"What did you mean when you said you could help him?" Ralf's mother asked as I shoved the stopper back into the bottle and tucked it in my pouch.

"I know a spell for tummy troubles. I read it in a book of magic."

Ralf's father snorted. "A spell! What are you, some kind of witch?"

"A witch in training, actually. I won't try the spell unless you want me to, so it's up to you."

The old king scratched his head with a claw and looked confused. "There's something I should tell you, something about dragon smoke. It's on the tip of my brain. If only I could remember."

Ralf groaned again. Clutching his tummy, he curled up into a tight little ball.

"Not now, Father!" said Flame Snorter. "If she can help Ralfie …"

"Do you want me to try?" I asked. Ralf's mother nodded and the little dragon's father frowned, but no one objected. I pointed my finger at Ralf, hoping the spell would work on dragons as well as humans. "Here goes," I said.

> Soothe the aching tummy,
> Quench the belly fire,
> Calm the quaking stomach,
> Douse the pain so dire.

As I lowered my finger, the room seemed to throb with a light so bright that I had to squeeze my eyes shut and cover them with my hands. There was a hissing sound like steam escaping from a cook pot, and Ralf sighed.

"Was that it?" said his father. "I expected a lot more."

"How do you feel?" I asked Ralf, but his color was already returning to its normal shade of blue.

Ralf blinked up at me and smiled. "I feel better. Thanks."

"Sorry about the fire dousing. It was part of the spell and I was afraid it might not work if I left that out."

"It doesn't matter," said the little dragon's mother. "As long as my baby feels better. He's too young to have a real fire yet anyway. When he's a little older, I'll start feeding him gunga beans and hot flami-peppers. That'll get his fire going."

"Mama! I'm not a baby anymore. And you know I don't like flami-peppers! You're not really going to make me eat them, are you?"

"Every day. And no more flowers for you, young dragon. You'll eat normal dragon food and nothing else. Have I made myself clear?"

"Yes, Mama," said Ralf.

"He's not the only one who eats things he shouldn't," I said, glancing at Eadric.

I'd grown used to the constant din outside the tent as the dragons scoured the area for us, only now it seemed to be getting louder. When I listened, I could make out one word above all the rest. *Humans* sounded like a name for evil when shouted by an angry mob of dragons. We were in serious trouble.

The Dragon King peered nearsightedly at Eadric and me and shook his head. "I can't believe I'm going to say this, but I think you two had better hide for a while. I'll try to head everyone off, but I can't help you if they find you. Even though you've done my family a mighty big favor, there's only so much I can do. Too bad you're humans, that's all I can say."

"What if they weren't humans?" asked Ralf. "What if they turned back into frogs? Then they could leave the tent and no one would notice them. You can do it, can't you, Emma?"

"That's a great idea, Ralf, but there's only one problem. I have to sneeze if we're going to turn back, and I don't know how to make myself do it."

"Isn't there some other way you can change? You fixed me with magic. Why don't you fix yourself?"

"When I fixed you, I used a spell I'd read in a book. I don't know any spells that would change me back."

"Then make one up," said Ralf. "Witches do that kind of thing, don't they?"

"I'm not very good at making up spells yet. They

never turn out quite right."

Grumble Belly pointed a sharp claw at my chest. "You mean you'd try your magic on our son but not on yourself?"

I glanced from dragon to dragon, hoping that at least one of them would understand. "It's not that I don't want to. I just can't." I swallowed hard when the adult dragons' eyes began to glow red and pink smoke trickled out of their nostrils. The temperature in the room seemed to be rising as swirling smoke filled the air and the smell of boiling cabbage became overpowering.

"I think you'd better try, Emma," said Eadric. "You don't have much of a choice."

"What about you, Eadric? I know how you feel about my spells. Whatever happens to me is going to happen to you, too. Are you sure you want me to do this?"

"I'm willing to risk it if you are. We've made it through so far, haven't we?"

I took a deep breath and nodded. "All right," I said with a halfhearted smile. "Just don't expect any great poetry."

"About that smoke," said the old dragon.

Flame Snorter glared at him. "Not now, Father. Give the girl a chance."

"This is important. I remember what I wanted to tell her, and it's something she'd better know. Young human," he said, turning to me, "do you see the dragon smoke in this tent? There's a lot more now than there was a minute ago."

"Yes, but—"

"Dragon smoke is pretty powerful stuff. We have our own special magic, and so does our smoke. After you've been breathing the smoke the way you have, if you try to cast a spell on yourself, it will change your magic, one way or another. Just thought I'd better warn you."

"What do you mean?" asked Eadric.

"If you're a friend to dragons, it'll make your magic stronger, but there aren't too many dragon friends around. If you're like most humans and wouldn't mind using your magic against us, you might lose your magic altogether. If that happens, I don't think you'll be leaving here alive. My family will try to help you, but those fellows outside aren't feeling too friendly. It's your choice, so make it a good one. Once you cast your spell, what happens next will be out of your hands."

I was frightened. Trying to sneak past the other dragons wasn't much of an option. I didn't want to die, and I didn't want to risk losing Eadric, who would do his best to protect me and end up getting himself killed. I didn't want to lose my magic, but the more I thought about it, the more I felt that I wasn't about to lose anything. I never had used my magic against dragons, and I had no intention of starting. Wouldn't that count for something?

When I tried to talk, the words seemed to stick in my

throat. I tried again, and they came out sounding funny to me, as if someone else was saying them. "I have to try the spell."

"All right," said the old dragon. "It's your decision."

I closed my eyes so that the dragons wouldn't distract me. It took me a minute to come up with something that I thought would work. When I was ready, I took a deep breath and said,

> I wish I might,
> I wish I may,
> Have the form
> I want today.
>
> Please let me choose
> Which it will be.
> No longer human
> Make it froggy.

The pink smoke seemed to be drawn to me, swirling around me in an ever-thickening cloud. Eadric and the dragons faded from sight and everything grew silent, leaving me alone in a world of shadows. Despite the heat, a chill walked up my spine and I shivered. With Eadric at my side, I had felt braver and more able to face whatever came, but now ... I tried to tell myself that everything would be fine. I had sworn that I'd never use my magic to hurt anyone, and as far as I knew, I'd never done anything worse than make a sea monster lose his teeth. Even then, he'd had another set coming in.

Something whispered at the edge of my hearing. I dug my nails into my palms and held my breath, straining to understand it. The sound came again, louder and more distinct. It was a voice, but it didn't belong to a human and it spoke no words that I could understand. Another voice joined in and then a third, and before I knew it, a chorus of voices surrounded me. They grew louder until suddenly they stopped, leaving me in silence once again.

Flashes of light broke through the smoke, red and yellow in a bed of dusky pink. *This is it,* I thought. *The dragons are going to turn me into charcoal.* I think I even forgot to breathe. Arrows of light with no beginning and no end shot through me as if I was no more substantial than a shadow. I heard soothing music and screams of terror, I tasted blood and sugar, smelled the stench of decay and the perfume of wildflowers. The arrows were cold and hot, they itched and burned and soothed ... and then they were gone.

I felt light-headed and as fresh and full of energy as if I'd just stepped from an invigorating swim in a cool mountain stream. My senses seemed sharper, my thoughts clearer. I knew that I'd turned into a frog, but I also knew that something bigger and far more important had happened to me. Whatever it was, I was no longer the same person I'd been just minutes before.

The smoke was almost gone when the noise of the Olympics returned. It was loud and harsh, yet I welcomed it as proof that everything was all right.

"Would you look at that!" exclaimed the Dragon King. "I should have known it would turn out like this after the way you helped our Ralfie!"

"You have a funny sort of glow now, Emma. I can see it when I squint my eyes real hard, like this," said Ralf, squeezing his eyes into little slits.

"When you said that her magic would be more powerful, how much of an increase did you mean?" asked Eadric.

"That depends on the person," said the Dragon King, "but it's usually quite substantial."

Although I didn't know what to say, Eadric didn't have the same problem. "That's just great!" he said, shaking his head. "You made some mistakes with your magic before, but I can imagine what you'll come up with now!"

A dark red dragon with jagged brow ridges lifted the tent flap and stuck his head inside. "Has anyone seen a pair of humans?" When his eyes fell on the Dragon King, he ducked his head, murmuring, "Sorry, Your Majesty. Didn't mean to intrude."

"Hmph," said Gargle Snout. "See that it doesn't

happen again. And take your search for humans else-where. There aren't any here."

The red dragon bowed and backed away, muttering apologies. When the flap had fallen closed, Eadric said, "I think we should leave before anything else happens."

Ralf rubbed his eyes and stifled a yawn. "I'll take you to find your sword—"

"You certainly will not!" said his mother. "You're not going anywhere with your friends now. You can hardly keep your eyes open, and I don't—"

"Mama!" wailed Ralf, his face crinkling.

"Don't worry, son," said his father. "I'll take your friends wherever they need to go. You listen to your mother, and I'll come see you when I get back."

"You don't mind?" the little dragon asked. "Because it's kind of far."

While Ralf gave directions to his father, I tried to think of a good reason for not going with the big drag-on. I knew and trusted Ralf, but his father was intimidat-ing even when he was trying to be friendly. I was opening my mouth to make some excuse when Grumble Belly picked us up, plopped us behind his neck ridge and trot-ted out of the tent.

"Goodbye!" yelled Ralf as the tent flap closed behind us.

"Goodbye!" I called back, but we were already airborne.

Twenty-two

Night had fallen while we were inside the tent, but the glow from the lava pit cast an otherworldly light over the arena. Instead of taking the tunnel through the mountain, Grumble Belly avoided the crowd by flying straight up. I was convinced that we were going to fall off his back at any moment, but he carried us safely through the mountain passes and over the forest, his great wings beating with a strong and steady rhythm.

It was a beautiful night with the stars twinkling overhead, the pale face of the moon nearly full and the crisp, clear air washing away the smell of Ralf's salve. If it hadn't been for the whump of the dragon's wings, it would have been silent as well.

Ralf must have given his father excellent directions, since the big dragon carried us directly to the trees where the spider's web had hung. It was dark in the woods, making it hard to see much of anything. The moment the dragon landed, Eadric sprang to the ground. I hopped off the dragon's back, too, not wanting to stay there by myself. "If you'll wait, I'll make a light," I said, hearing Eadric stumble in the dark.

"Don't bother," said Grumble Belly. He closed his eyes and concentrated until his stomach made a grumbling sort of sound, like an old man makes when his bones are aching. Taking a deep breath, the dragon exhaled with his mouth partly closed, letting out a thin tongue of flame and the now-familiar cabbagey smell. The flame created enough light to illuminate the nearby ground all the way to the lowest branches of the closest trees. It went out when he inhaled, lighting again with his next breath, illuminating the area in a pulse of light, dark, light, dark. It was helpful, but not perfect since I could see Eadric for a moment, and then he disappeared as the flame went out.

"Ow!" said Eadric. I could see him now, standing by a tree and rubbing his forehead, apparently having run into a branch. Staring at the ground by his feet, he said, "I know Ferdy is around here somewhere."

"Grumble Belly," I said, taking a step back when the dragon's huge head swung around to face me, "would you be able to carry us if we were humans?"

"Easily," the dragon answered.

"Then I think it's time we stopped being frogs." Since it had worked so well the first time, I used the same spell again—with a small adjustment.

I wish I might,
I wish I may,
Have the form
I want today.

Let me choose
Which it will be.
A human form
Is right for me.

My magic felt different now. While it had taken a lot of effort and concentration before and I had to hope I was saying the right thing each time, now I knew when it was right, and it wasn't just because the spell was similar to the one I'd said in the tent. Now I could see what effect my words would have before I said them. This time when I said the spell, the change took place in an instant and I didn't feel queasy afterward. Powerful magic definitely had its advantages.

While Eadric shuffled through the dead leaves, searching for Ferdy, I tried to remember where he'd been standing when we turned into frogs. I knew where I'd been and he'd been right. "What's this?" I asked when my foot hit something hard. I knelt down to brush the leaves aside and uncovered his sword, only a few feet from where he'd been looking. Eadric reached for Ferdy, then stood up, holding the sword at arm's length.

"I'm sorry I left you, Ferdy," said Eadric. "I didn't mean to. Please forgive me."

Ferdy didn't stay silent for long.

> I'm never one to hold a grudge.
> I never can stay mad.
> I'll never be the kind to judge.
> To see you makes me glad.

"Ferdy's better than a faithful hound," I said. "A sword that forgiving won't chew up your shoes when it's starving for attention."

"He is a good sword, isn't he? I'd say he wasn't such a bad purchase after all."

The trip home took only a few minutes. We were within sight of the castle when Grumble Belly said, "I'd drop you at your front door, but that would bring out all the guards. Is there somewhere out of the way where I can let you off?"

"Over there," I said, pointing to the tower on the left. "That's where my aunt lives. She won't mind if we use her window. In fact, she'd probably like to meet you."

"Another time, perhaps." Grumble Belly dipped one wing and swerved toward the tower, gliding up to the window silently.

"Thanks for the ride," I said, jumping onto the ledge. Eadric checked to make sure that he had his possessions with him before following me through the window. "Thanks," he said.

Grumble Belly smiled. "You saved my son's life and became his friends. Here," he said, snapping off the tip of an already cracked claw and depositing it on the window ledge. "If you ever need me, hold this in your left hand and call my name. Dragons don't forget their friends."

Eadric and I stood by the window, watching the dragon's silhouette winging through the night sky. A shout went up from the guard on the next tower, but Grumble Belly was already too far away for an arrow to reach.

I picked up the dragon's claw and tucked it in my pouch, intending to examine it in the daylight.

The door to the storage room creaked open and a small head peeked out. "Is it gone?" Li'l whispered, peering around the room.

"Yes, Li'l," I said. "The dragon's gone."

"Thank goodness!" said the little bat. Li'l leaned forward and peered at me. "So, did you get the dragon's breath and the feather?"

"We got it all! I have the dragon's breath right here," I said, patting my pouch.

"And here are the feathers," Eadric said, handing them to me. I was carrying them to Grassina's workbench when he pointed toward the back of the room and whispered, "Who's that?"

A pale figure seemed to be floating toward us, and I

thought it must be one of the castle ghosts until she stepped in the puddle of moonlight shining through the window. It was my mother, her hair streaming loose around her shoulders and down her back, her long, white gown brushing her ankles and reaching past her fingertips.

I pointed at the witches' lights, lighting a half dozen or so.

"You're back," she said, sounding relieved. "Is Grassina with you?"

"You mean she isn't here? But she knows we have to turn Haywood back within the next few hours!"

"Haywood! I wish I'd never heard that name. He's made her forget everything, and now she isn't even here when we need her so desperately."

"What happened? Is something wrong?"

"Of course something's wrong! King Beltran's army has almost reached the border. Your father is waiting for him there. If Grassina doesn't help your father, Beltran's wizard can destroy our entire army before a single arrow is shot. Emeralda, you told me that you'd learned a little magic. Do you know how to locate Grassina? We need her back here right away!"

"I'll see what I can do." It occurred to me that my mother had to be truly desperate to accept my magic so suddenly, which made me want to help even more. I searched Grassina's workbench for her dragon scale, but she must have taken it with her again. "I can use this," I said, finding her old far-seeing ball. Although she had a newer and more powerful one, that seemed to be missing as well.

"Eadric, help me find something personal of Grassina's that I can use to locate her. Try checking her comb or her pillow. If we're lucky, her cleaning spell missed a hair or two."

Unfortunately, Grassina's spell was too thorough. We didn't find any of her hair, but we did find a clump of Haywood's fur on the window seat.

"This will have to do," I said. "We'll see if we can find Haywood and hope that Grassina is nearby."

"I don't understand," said Eadric. "If you can find Haywood this way, why didn't Grassina try it? It has to be easier than whatever she's been doing."

"It depends on the distance involved," I said. "This won't be easy if he's too far away. My aunt is a powerful witch, but this may be too hard even for her. And remember, she had to eliminate all those false trails."

I already knew what I was going to say when I set the fur on Grassina's workbench and placed the far-seeing ball on top of it.

> In the day or in the night,
> In the dark or in the light,
> Show me where the otter's gone,
> Show me now before the dawn.

An image formed inside the ball, fuzzy at first, but it grew more distinct as we watched. The sun was high over a riverbank where an otter, his fur wet and shiny, slipped and slid across the mud. A shadowy figure was chasing him, but the otter was too wild to catch. Twisting around as the figure reached out, he snapped and bit, then scampered toward the water as the figure fell back, nursing an injured hand.

"Is that Grassina?" Eadric asked, squinting at the image. "Why is she so hard to see?"

"Because she isn't the one I asked to see," I said.

"Can you contact her?" asked my mother.

"I can do better than that." I was feeling stronger and more confident in my magic than I ever had before, and making up spells no longer seemed such a challenge.

"Step back," I said, "and stay out of the way. This might be messy." Taking the ball in my hands, I turned to face the center of the chamber.

Bring the otter to this room
So that he can be a groom.
Bring my aunt who's chasing him,
Keep them safe in life and limb.

The splat of something wet and heavy hitting the floor made me jump. Haywood had landed first, tumbling across my aunt's beautiful carpet and smearing it with mud. Grassina appeared next, sprawling on the floor with a whoosh as the air was knocked out of her. Stunned, she lay still for a moment, and I began to worry that she'd been hurt. She was shaky when she stood up, but I thought she looked fine until I noticed the blood dripping from her hand.

"Oh, my!" exclaimed my aunt, staring at us in surprise. "How did that happen?"

"Emma used a spell," Eadric began.

Grassina looked at him as if he was crazy. "Who?"

"Emma," Eadric said again. "She found you in that ball thing, and then she said a spell to bring you here. Queen Chartreuse said she needed you, so Emma—"

"Emma couldn't possibly do that. I don't know anyone who could bring two people over such a distance. There must be—"

Haywood was acting like any wild thing suddenly let loose indoors. He panicked, his claws digging into the carpet as he scurried from one end of the room to the other, trying to find a way out. I stopped listening to Grassina when he ran into the table holding the crystalline bouquet. The table fell over with a crash, and the bouquet would have been smashed on the floor if Eadric hadn't launched himself across the room, catching it with both hands.

"Good catch!" I said, and darted after the frantic otter. I chased him into the corner of the room, which I decided wasn't a good idea when he bared his teeth and growled. Backing away one step at a time, I pointed my finger at him and said,

Send this otter to the pond
Where I first met Eadric.
Do not let the otter leave,
By free will or by magic.

The instant I finished the spell, Haywood disappeared, leaving behind mud and the musky scent of wet otter. I heard Grassina gasp, and when I turned around, she was staring at me as if I'd grown another head.

"I'm sorry, but he couldn't stay here," I said. "He's too wild to keep inside."

"I know. I would have done the same thing. I just can't believe how much you've changed. The Emma I used to know couldn't have done that. And if you were really the one to bring us here—"

"She was," my mother said, surprising me by looking proud. "Now hold still and let me look at that hand." Muttering to herself, my mother made Grassina sit down and began to dab at her wound using water from the pitcher and a clean cloth. "You two can talk later," Mother added. "Grassina has to go help Limelyn. She said that when she came back—"

My aunt frowned at her. "I said that I'd help him

after I took care of Haywood. I still have to turn my darling back, and I don't have much time."

"But Beltran's troops have almost reached the border," said Mother. "His wizard—"

"Isn't going to do anything until morning. Olebald isn't very powerful, so he needs to see what he's doing. He'll wait for daylight. As I said before, I'll go directly there once Haywood is changed back. Now if you don't mind, I have a lot to do."

"Do you swear you will on your honor as the Green Witch?" my mother asked, tightening the bandage that she was wrapping around her sister's hand.

"*Ow!*" yelped Grassina. "Yes, I swear! Now, get some sleep. You'll need to be rested for Greater Greensward's victory celebration." Taking my mother by the arm, Grassina led her to the door.

"All right, as long as you swear." Mother said, letting her sister push her across the threshold.

Twenty-three

*G*rassina gestured, and more witches' lights began to glow, the light soft and diffuse. Eadric's stomach rumbled, and a crimson fog floated around the room. He blushed, his face turning nearly the same color as the fog.

"Eadric ate the seeds inside the magic beans," I said, certain that that was all the explanation my aunt needed.

Grassina shook her head sadly, although a smile tugged at the corners of her mouth. "You shouldn't have eaten those seeds, Eadric. Those were old magic beans whose magic gets stronger with age. Every month for the rest of your life your problem will return when the moon is full."

My grandfather was known as Aldrid the Wise, my father was Limelyn the Courageous, yet the man I might marry one day could be called Eadric the Flatulent. Eadric groaned when his stomach grumbled, and I couldn't keep from smiling. What a time to realize that I really *wanted* to marry him!

"I think I'll go down to the kitchen," Eadric said, heading for the door. "It's been a while since we ate last. Emma, are you coming?"

"No, I need to stay and help Aunt Grassina." I settled into my usual chair in front of the fireplace. Grassina joined me in the other chair, and we waited until Eadric had closed the door behind him. When my aunt sighed, I knew that something was wrong.

"Father will be all right, won't he?" I asked.

"Oh, yes. This has nothing to do with your father. It's just that I'm not sure I'm doing the right thing about Haywood."

"What are you saying? Don't you want to get him back the way he was?"

"Yes, of course I do, or at least I think I do. But what if we've changed so much that we don't like each other anymore? Or what if we discover that we've fallen out of love? I'm no longer the young girl who fell in love with the romantic young wizard in training. I've had a lot of time to think about this. It took me much longer than I thought it would to find Haywood. Then when I did, Mother had made him forget that he was ever human, just as she said she would. He was happy as an otter, happier than most men ever are. What right did I have to bring him back here to life as a human?"

"He was happy as an otter because of Grandmother's spell, you know that. But he'll be happier with

259

you. I saw the way he looked at you when you found him the other day. He'd even carved your name in the bark of an old oak, although it must have been terribly difficult for an otter. He loves you, Aunt Grassina, and if he was in his right mind, he'd tell you so."

Grassina held up her hand, showing me the wrapping stained with blood. "He bit me, Emma! When I finally found him, he bit me like a wild animal!"

"It was Grandmother's spell. I know the real Haywood loves you!"

Grassina sighed again. "Perhaps you're right, Emma. I know so little about affairs of the heart. It's been so long." She closed her eyes and rubbed her temples as if in pain, but when she looked at me again, she seemed a little more cheery. "If we're going through with this, we'd better get busy. Dawn will be here before we know it."

While Grassina started toward her room to fetch the items from the silver chest, I reached into my pouch for the bottle of dragon's breath. I was about to take it out when I heard a rustling by the window. I gasped when Grandmother shot through the opening. Hopping off her broom, she pointed a finger at Grassina. "There you are! Did you find him?"

Grassina turned her head and glared. "What are you doing here?"

"I've come to keep you from making a terrible mistake!"

"The only mistake I've made was letting you near Haywood again," said Grassina. "I should have known better than to ask you for help."

"Is that any way to talk to your mother?"

"In your case, yes. Now please leave."

Grandmother muttered something as she squinted, her tiny eyes nearly disappearing in a mass of wrinkles. Grassina must have guessed what her mother was up to, because she put her hand in front of her face and recited something very fast. With a high-pitched whistle, Grandmother's spell bounced off Grassina and attached itself to its creator. Furious, Grandmother clawed at her lips, tearing away strands of something thick and white that seemed to writhe in her hands.

"Why, you little pipsqueak!" shrilled my grandmother once she'd uncovered her mouth. "You restore Henry and your life will change forever!"

"I hope so, Mother, and his name is *Haywood!*"

"This is for your own good, daughter!" screamed Grandmother as she hurled a ball of the tangled white strands at Grassina.

My aunt ducked, and the ball splattered against the wall behind her. "Mother, I'm warning you, you aren't going to change my mind."

"Let's bring Howard here and we'll see what he thinks." Grandmother muttered something and made clockwise circles with her hand. A puff of orange smoke

261

clouded the corner of the room, and when it cleared, Haywood stood blinking at the light. Grandmother spoke again, and a dozen wasps buzzed through the window, heading straight for the otter. If I hadn't known the strength of my spell, I might have been convinced.

"Haywood!" screamed Grassina as he snapped and batted at the wasps. Without thought for her own safety, my aunt rushed to help him. The moment Grassina turned her back, Grandmother pointed at her and muttered. It must have been a binding spell, for my aunt froze in midstep. Her body trembled as she fought to break the spell.

"Harvey isn't worth the breath it takes to say his name," my grandmother shrilled. "I don't know why you're being so thickheaded!"

"Because she loves him!" I said, surprising even myself. I couldn't bear it any longer. My grandmother had done everything she could to stand in the way of true love, and even that hadn't been enough for her. "You may have fooled Grassina, but I know that's not Haywood. He's still right where I put him, and that's where he'll stay until we're ready. Your tricks aren't going to work with me, so you might as well stop now."

Grandmother grumbled and waved her arm. The false images of the otter and the wasps began to fade.

"What you're doing is wrong, Grandmother!" I continued. "Can't you see that they should be together?"

My grandmother's eyes flashed. "I see. You've learned a little magic, so you think you can interfere. Well, this is none of your business. This is between my daughter and me." With a flick of her fingers, silver sparks shot from their tips, sizzling as if they burned the air.

Keep it simple, I thought, and a spell formed in my mind almost effortlessly.

> The wind must blow,
> It can't be slow.
> Put out each spark
> And leave no mark.

A sudden gust of wind shook the tapestries on the walls, whipped my hair about my head, blew the loose parchments off Grassina's desk and turned the sparks into fizzling dust that fell harmlessly to the floor when the wind died down.

"Very nice!" exclaimed Grandmother, and suddenly I had the impression that she was pleased. "Now how about this?" I was surprised to see her vanish, but even more surprised that I could still sense her presence in the room.

"I know you're here, Grandmother. Hasn't this gone on long enough?" When she didn't answer. I said, "Fine. If that's the way you're going to act, let's try this."

let each life here
Give off a glow,
To help me learn
What I must know.

My skin tingled, and the air around me began to shimmer while a golden aura formed around my aunt and Li'l. I blinked, and when I looked again I saw a glowing light roughly my grandmother's size and shape. The light moved, and I heard my grandmother laugh. "Very good! Maybe we'll make a witch of you yet."

Somehow, what had started as a fight between my aunt and my grandmother had ended up feeling like a test for me. From the tone of my grandmother's voice, it seemed that I had passed.

A blue mist floated through the door, and my grandfather materialized in the middle of the room. "Back so soon, Olivene? You stay away for years, and now you visit twice in one week?"

Grandmother reappeared with a small pop. "Mind your own business, you old fool," she said, her bristling eyebrows drawn together in a V. "This is between me and my granddaughter."

"She's my granddaughter, too. Leave her alone, Olivene. She doesn't need you interfering in her life."

"And I don't need your advice, Aldrid. I was leaving anyway. I've already said what I wanted to say and learned what I wanted to learn." Grandmother smiled at me, then turned to waggle her fingers at Grassina. My aunt's foot hit the floor with a thump, and she staggered a step or two.

"Then why are you still here?" asked Grandfather.

"I'm not," Grandmother said. Hopping onto her waiting broom, she flew around the room, cackling like an old hen and making us duck to avoid her. When she flew out the window, a full moon framed her silhouette.

Grandfather shook his head. "That woman gets crazier every time I see her."

"I heard that!" Grandmother shouted over her shoulder, her voice fading with distance.

"Thanks for stopping by, Father, although I could have handled it myself," said Grassina. "I was running through the standard releases for binding spells. I would have broken it soon, and then I would have taken care of Mother."

"I know, but I wanted to see her, even if it was just for a minute. She has the personality of a crazed she-bear, but I miss her just the same. Nice or nasty, your grandmother has always been the most exciting woman I've ever known. It wasn't her fault that she turned mean. Good night, ladies. Come visit me when you can."

Grassina waited until Grandfather had dematerialized, then raised her eyebrows and turned to me. "So what have you been doing? Your magic has improved more than I would have thought possible in such a short time."

"It was the magic miasma at the Dragon Olympics," I said. "It seems that when you do magic—"

"Never mind," she said, shaking her head and smiling. "It sounds like a long story, and I want you to tell me all about it when we have time. Right now, we'd better see to Haywood. The sun will be up before we know it."

I followed my aunt to her workbench. Taking out a small clay bowl, Grassina dropped in one of Surely's feathers, Nastia Nautica's gossamer hair and the husk of a magic bean. Li'l watched every move, her head swiveling back and forth. I handed Grassina the bottle of dragon's breath. She shook it, then said,

> Solids become liquids,
> Liquids turn to gas.
> Reverse the process
> With my next pass.

> Make this gas a liquid
> For an hour or two.
> Return it to its present form
> When its work is through.

When she waved the bottle over the bowl once more, the contents sparkled, becoming so bright that I had to look away.

"I find that liquids are much easier to use in some

circumstances, gases in others. In this case," she said, holding up the bottle so I could see the blue-green fluid inside, "a liquid is handier. Now watch."

Slowly tilting the bottle, Grassina poured in three drops, waited a moment, then poured in another three. My heart beat one, two, three times, then the liquid dragon's breath grew hot, bubbling like the lava in the dragon's pool, and the feather, the hair and the bean husk curled into tight little balls before dissolving. The liquid, now a creamy blue, was light and frothy with bubbles rising and falling.

"Good," said Grassina, setting a lid on the bowl. "Now we're all set." Recapping the bottle, she handed it to me before picking up the potion. "Keep that bottle safe. There's no telling when you might need it next, and it was probably very difficult to get."

You have no idea, I thought, but when I saw her secret little smile, I decided that maybe she did after all.

Twenty-four

Dressed in heavy cloaks against the early morning chill, Grassina, Eadric and I hurried along the path to the swamp, lighting our way with torches. The sky was already growing brighter when we reached the pond. It wasn't a terribly large pond, but it had always been my favorite. I loved the stand of cattails at the far end, the willows trailing their lance-shaped leaves in the water, and the wash of gravel where I had often stood to survey my own, small kingdom. Haywood was floating on his back in the morning mist, seeming as if he didn't have a care in the world.

Grassina wasn't about to wait any longer. Holding out her hands, she called,

> Come to me, my darling.
> Come to me, my friend.
> When you have sipped
> The drink I hold,

Your feral life will end.

As if in a trance, Haywood rolled over onto his belly and swam toward Grassina, his liquid brown eyes never leaving her face. Uncovering the bowl, Grassina crouched by the water's edge. When Haywood's paws touched the mud of the bank, she tilted the bowl, pouring its contents into his open mouth.

Haywood blinked up at Grassina. Gradually, more mist rose from the water around him, and his edges began to blur. The dark, furry form that was Haywood grew longer, his head and body larger, his tail disappearing altogether.

I glanced at Grassina. Although her eyes had been troubled just moments before, they were now lit with the purest joy I had ever seen. She gazed into Haywood's eyes; her face softened. As the mist dissolved, I could see that Haywood was human again. A middle-aged man, he was dressed in clothes twenty years out of style. His sandy brown hair was tinged with gray, his brown eyes warm and friendly. From the way he looked at Grassina, it was plain that his memory had returned and that he still adored my aunt.

They reached toward each other with trembling hands. Their faces seemed to glow with happiness, and I felt my throat tighten when they leaned toward each other and kissed. I was still watching them when a breeze sprang up, chasing away the last of the mist and bringing with it a shower of rose petals, pink, red, purple and every shade in between. They drifted around us in a gentle blanket, filling the air with their sweet scent.

I was brushing a few clinging petals from my face when I felt something hard rub against my cheek. I glanced at my hand and was startled to find Grassina's green leaf ring on my finger. "Why is this—" I began, and then I heard someone gasp. I turned back to Grassina and Haywood. The breeze had died, leaving them covered with petals. Jerking his hands away from Grassina, Haywood struggled to back up, but his feet slid out from under him and he landed in deeper water with a splash.

I wondered what could have caused the look of horror on his face, and then Grassina turned around, the petals fell away, and I knew. No longer the beautiful woman I had known my entire life, she had become just like my grandmother. The curse we'd all feared, the curse the fairy had put on my ancestor, Hazel, had taken its toll, turning Grassina's glorious auburn hair stringy and black, her well-shaped nose so long that it almost reached her jutting chin. She had more hairy warts on her face than I had toes on my feet, and her fingers were bent and gnarled.

It was the rose petals, I thought. *Grandmother must have added that to the spell she cast on Haywood. She's had her way after all.*

"What are you pea brains gawking at?" Grassina asked, her voice as scratchy as a rusty knife.

"You've changed," I squeaked.

"Of course I've changed, fly breath. I've gotten a whole lot smarter. The wedding's off. I wouldn't marry fur-boy if he was the last wizard in the swamp. Now go away and stop bothering me. I've got to get out of these disgusting clothes and into something more suitable."

Grassina stormed off in the direction of the castle. Dumbstruck, we watched her stomp away, then turned and looked at each other.

"What just happened?" asked Haywood, water dribbling from his clothes as he slogged his way out of the pond. "Where's my Grassina? I thought that was Grassina, but then that hag ... Did that woman do something to her? Is she in danger?"

"No, I don't think so," I said, and gave him a brief description of the curse. His expression changed from horrified to woeful as I explained what must have happened. "That woman was your Grassina, at least until the curse took hold. I don't think she's anyone's Grassina now."

"There must be something we can do about it! You're training to be a witch, and I was studying wizardry before Olivene changed me. Between the two of us, we should be able to think of something. What did the curse say, exactly?"

"That's just it. The only one who would know is the fairy who said it, but we don't even know who that was. It's hopeless." The enormity of what had happened finally began to sink in. The woman who had been the kindest, most caring person in my life was gone, replaced by a horrible crone. Fighting back tears, I could feel my throat close up, making it hard to speak. "I'm sorry that this happened. If I hadn't insisted that we see my grandmother—"

"I'd still be an otter and Grassina and I would have spent the rest of our lives trying to find a solution. And as soon as we did, Grassina would have turned nasty anyway." Haywood grimaced and rubbed the back of his neck, turning his head from side to side.

"You'll be stiff for a while," I said, "but it won't be long before you're back to normal."

"Normal, eh? For twenty-three years normal was being an otter. It wasn't a bad life, either. The only thing I really missed was Grassina."

"I know. We never thought that my grandmother would go to such lengths."

"Olivene must have hated me even more than I realized, although I don't know why. If I could get my hands on her now, though, I'd give her plenty of reason."

"That would only make things worse. Why don't you go to the castle? Cook will give you something to eat, and I'll talk to my parents. I'm sure we can find a place for you to stay until you decide what you want to do."

Haywood took a step, his legs shaking beneath him. "Thanks," he said. "This is going to take some getting used to."

While I probably should have helped Haywood get to the castle, I couldn't make myself go back just yet. I was angry at my grandmother for her spell and at Grassina for succumbing to it, but mostly I was angry at myself. Turning back to the pond, I glared at Eadric, although I knew that none of it was his fault. "I can't believe this!" I said. "Why did I have to be such an inter-fering busybody who couldn't stay out of other people's business? If only I hadn't been so convincing when Grassina wanted to give up. If only I hadn't encouraged her to ask my grandmother for help. If only I hadn't brought them back together in the first place. I should have known my grandmother would do something like this!"

"What about your father?" asked Eadric, a puzzled expression on his face. "Isn't Grassina going to help him?"

"Oh, no!" I said. "She was supposed to go now, wasn't she? What are we going to do?"

"What do you mean? Just because she looks differ-ent, it doesn't mean that she's lost her ability to—"

"That's true!" I said, and began to run. "I'm sure she's just forgotten." When I saw my aunt up ahead, using a stick to whack the heads off daisies while she walked, I shouted, "Grassina! Wait for me!" Instead of waiting, my aunt began to walk faster.

I jerked my hem from the grasp of clutching brambles and hurried after Grassina, finally catching up with her on the path that led into one of the kitchen gardens. "What do you want?" she asked, glaring down the length of her long nose at me.

"My father!" I gasped, out of breath from running. "You have to go help him!"

Grassina sniffed loudly. "No, I don't. It's no longer my responsibility. I don't have to do anything I don't want to."

"But the Green Witch—"

"That's right. It's up to the Green Witch, and that's you now. See this ring?" she asked, grabbing my wrist and twisting it to get a better look at my hand. "It means that you have to protect the kingdom." Her eyes glittered when she shoved my hand away and started up the path.

"But I don't know what to do!" I wailed.

Without stopping or turning around, she shouted, "You'll figure it out!"

Eadric caught up with me while I stood open-mouthed, watching Grassina stomp off. "Is she going to help your father?" he asked.

I shook my head. "No. She says that I'm the Green Witch now, so it's up to me." I held out my hand and showed him the ring.

Eadric's jaw dropped. "You're the Green Witch? You've got to be kidding!"

The dumbfounded look on his face was almost insulting. "It's not that hard to believe! I'm sure I can do it. I just have to figure out how."

"You mean she didn't tell you?"

"No," I said, "and I don't think the job comes with a list of instructions. Just give me a moment to think!"

"Sure." Eadric stepped back a pace and raised both hands in the air as if surrendering. "Go right ahead."

I didn't know what I should do. Because of me, my father had been left without any magical defense. I was sure that Grassina would have known exactly what steps to take before she'd changed, but even if she still knew, she wasn't about to tell me. And what about my grand-mother? She had seemed awfully pleased with my improved magical abilities. Maybe she really had been testing me. Maybe she was trying to see if I was good enough to be the next Green Witch. She had to have known what would happen when Grassina kissed Haywood, so maybe Grandmother wanted to see what I was capable of doing before letting her daughter have her way. I don't know what would have happened if I hadn't been good enough, yet the fact that the ring had ended up on my finger meant a great deal to me. Even so, just because I was the new Green Witch didn't mean that I knew how to help my father. *If only I had some help,* I thought, and suddenly I knew what to do. I smiled, glad that I hadn't had time to clean out my pouch.

"He said to call on him if I ever needed to," I said, reaching into the cloth bag.

Eadric frowned. "Who said that?"

Taking the broken fragment of dragon claw in my left hand, I yelled, "Grumble Belly!"

"You didn't have to shout," said Eadric. "It was just a simple question."

"I wasn't shouting at you; I was calling him. I hope it doesn't take him long to get here."

I tried to wait patiently, but Eadric kept muttering things like "stupid idea" and "waste of time." "Listen," he said finally, "why don't I get Bright Country? The sooner we start—"

There was a clap like thunder, and Grumble Belly dropped out of the sky, his shadow gliding across the pond. His leathery wings made a rustling sound as he landed beside us. "When I said you could call on me, I didn't mean right away. Dragons need to sleep sometime, you know."

"I didn't think I'd have to call you this soon, but everything has changed." I explained that I'd become the Green Witch and that my father was counting on me. "And you were the only one I could think of to ask for help."

"What am I, the invisible prince?" muttered Eadric. "You could have asked me."

The dragon sighed. "I'll do what I can. Is he coming, too?" Using a blunted claw, Grumble Belly rapped Eadric on the chest, nearly knocking him to the ground.

"Of course," I said, climbing up onto the dragon's scaly shoulder. "I always need Eadric."

Twenty-five

Greater Greensward is a fairly large kingdom, but it didn't take long to cross it on the back of a full-grown dragon. I was familiar with the border, having visited it many times, so when we didn't hit the correct spot immediately, I told Grumble Belly to head north.

Long before we saw the armies, we spotted dragons circling in the sky. There were three of the scaly beasts, all a vivid orange shading to crimson and all larger than Grumble Belly.

"Do you recognize them?" I asked our dragon friend.

"I've never seen them before. They must not be from around here. Siblings, probably, since they're all the same color and their shading matches."

I studied the dragons as we flew closer. They didn't look at all like the dragons I'd seen at the Olympics. Even the way they moved seemed odd; the sweep of their wings was jerky and the way they turned their heads too abrupt.

"Hello!" Grumble Belly called, but the trio of dragons ignored him.

We finally passed the last of the trees in what had seemed to be an endless forest. Below us lay farmland already taken over by the two armies. They faced each other in straight rows with only a few hundred yards and a trickling stream between them. Both sides appeared to be waiting for a signal.

"I'd better see my father first," I said, and leaned forward to tap Grumble Belly's shoulder. "Can you take us down now, please? I want to talk to the king in the green armor."

My father had to calm his plunging horse when Grumble Belly landed beside him. When he finally stood still enough that we could talk, Father turned to me. "So, Emma, I expected to see Grassina. What are *you* doing here, and *what* are you riding?"

"Grassina finally fell victim to the family curse, so I'm the new Green Witch. This is our friend, Grumble Belly. He's helping us."

"Grumble Belly, huh?" Father said, eyeing the enormous dragon. "You say he's a friend? Then he isn't under a spell?" I noticed that my father's hand had moved toward his sword, but when I nodded, he took his hand away. "Someday you'll have to tell me how you two met. And you mean to say that Grassina acts like Olivene now?"

I nodded. "And Haywood is a man again."

"I'll have a lot to get used to, won't I?" he said. "What do you plan to do, Emma?"

"Whatever you need." I glanced at the knights trying to calm their frightened horses. "But I think we'd better get back in the air before we scare away your army."

"Then see what you can do about those orange dragons. We can handle Beltran's troops, but not while dragons are attacking."

When Grumble Belly leaped into the air, he headed straight for the other army. The men in the front lines looked like peasants fresh from the fields. Wearing stiffened leather for armor, and carrying pitchforks and axes for weapons, I didn't think they stood much of a chance against my father's trained soldiers. Beltran had kept his own trained men toward the back and it looked like he was there as well, seated on a black horse behind the foot soldiers and the mounted knights. I decided that another, trimmer figure seated on a white horse to his right must be Prince Jorge since they were dressed almost alike. Helmeted and wearing suits of chain mail, the triple griffins of their family crest decorated their horse's trappings as well as their shields, but while the king wore black, Jorge was dressed in shining silver.

Another man sat astride a gray horse to the left of the king. Taller than Beltran or Jorge, he had flowing white hair and wore a long black cape. His face was uncovered, and from where I sat, he looked like he might be handsome, although not as handsome as the prince. When the man gestured at the dragons, I realized that he must be the wizard. *That can't be Olebald,* I thought. *He doesn't look anything like Olefat.* Realizing that Grassina must have been mistaken, I swallowed hard and tried to ignore the tight feeling in my chest. This was no incompetent wizard who would be easy to defeat.

My father sat at the head of his mounted knights, his visor raised as he watched the dragons descend. The beasts flamed and my father's men cried out. Horses reared and pranced, creating havoc in my father's ranks.

"Beltran's wizard must be controlling those dragons," said Eadric. "It would take a strong wizard to control three dragons at once, wouldn't it, Grumble Belly?"

The dragon snorted, and a sour puff of air wafted past us. "I've never met a wizard who could control one dragon so completely, let alone three. Dragons don't normally involve themselves in the affairs of men. He must be a powerful wizard indeed."

I watched as the dragons swooped and veered, flying low over my father's men and scattering the more skittish horses. Some of the foot soldiers broke ranks and ran, leaving the lines in even greater disorder. The dragons were fearsome enough, yet they seemed so odd.

"Let's challenge them," I said to Grumble Belly, "and let them know we're here."

"But there are three of them, and they're the biggest dragons I've ever seen," said Eadric.

I sniffed the air. "That doesn't matter. Do you smell boiled cabbage?"

Eadric grunted. "What are you talking about? Even I can't think of food at a time like this."

The orange dragons swerved and came back toward my father's troops. Beating their wings in unison, they swooped low over the cowering men. Horses screamed and fought their reins, and a full third of my father's army disappeared into the forest.

"You're right!" exclaimed Grumble Belly. "I don't smell anything even though they've been flaming."

"Exactly! Now, how about that challenge?"

"Cover your ears!" Grumble Belly's sides expanded as he inhaled. The roar was deafening, even with my fingers stuck in my ears. My father's remaining troops looked up, but they stood their ground and watched us with their swords raised and their bowstrings taut. Beltran's men looked surprised, and I saw fear in the way his foot soldiers drew closer together. The three dragons' movements became jerkier for a moment, then they turned and headed toward us.

When Grumble Belly flew higher, the three orange dragons rose to meet him, flaming long before they were within reach. After seeing how far a dragon could flame at the Olympics, I thought their flames looked meager.

"Watch out!" shouted Eadric. "Those flames may not hurt you, Grumble Belly, but we'll be burned to cinders."

I shook my head. "I don't think so, but you can close your eyes if you want."

"Close my eyes? What good will that do?"

"Sometimes your eyes can trick you even though your brain knows the truth," I said.

A moment later, the flames from the orange dragons reached us. I felt nothing, however, except the rush of the wind against my face as Grumble Belly beat his wings and soared.

"What's going on?" asked Eadric.

"Watch and learn," I said, and recited a quick and easy spell.

> Let all that's false
> Now disappear.
> We do not want
> To see it here.

The orange dragons flickered, then one by one they faded away, leaving nothing behind to mark that they had ever been there. "They weren't real," I said.

An excited shout went up from my father's troops, echoed by a groan of despair from Beltran's men. Suddenly a lone horseman broke away from the enemies' lines, galloping toward the closest trees. Beltran's wizard was kicking his heels into his horse's sides to make it go faster. "Follow that man," I told Grumble Belly, and an instant later we were passing over the heads of my father's foes. Drawing closer, I was surprised to see that the wizard was bald-headed and pleasant-faced; he looked a lot like Olefat. Just like the three dragons, the wizard's appearance had been a lie.

Grumble Belly was almost directly over him when Olebald turned and looked up. I was too far away to hear what he said, but I saw his hands wave and suddenly a small dark cloud appeared above us. Thunder rumbled in its depths and a bolt of lightning zigzagged through the sky.

"Hold on tight!" bellowed Grumble Belly as he tucked his wings and dove. Eadric reached around me and we both clutched the dragon's ridge, our knuckles white from pressure. The first bolt missed us, but the second hit the dragon's tail, jolting him with a surge. He plummeted, tumbling head over heels. The lightning had stunned us as well, and we fell from his back, unable to control our muscles enough to hold on. I couldn't hear anything but the ringing in my ears, although I must have screamed, since I made my throat sore. I was too numb to think, let alone say a spell, and Eadric and I would have been killed if Grumble Belly hadn't come to his senses and beaten the air with his wings, bringing him level beneath us. He caught us with his skull, a lumpy and uncomfortable place to land. As the air woofed out of me, I knew I'd bear the bruises for days.

Although I couldn't hear, my head cleared as Eadric helped me back to my seat on Grumble Belly's neck. I realized that even though the cloud was shrinking as it leaked rain, it probably still held enough energy to shoot more lightning. Bending toward the dragon's neck, I shouted, "Would you mind heating up that cloud?"

"I'd be delighted!" said Grumble Belly, and with a blast of flame, he turned the cloud into steam, which quickly dissipated in the clear blue sky.

Before Olebald could aim his magic at us again, I pointed at him and said,

> Go to the isle of sun-warmed sand,
> Where memories were taken.
> Stay there till your king's gone home,
> His urge to fight forsaken.

A tiny whirlwind sprang up under the horse's hooves, growing until it engulfed both horse and rider. I watched as the swirling wind rose from the ground and carried them away.

When Eadric spoke, his voice was faint in my still ringing ears. "It looks as though the fighting has started without us."

While fleeing the storm cloud, we had flown over the forest, leaving the battlefield behind. I turned and saw that the archers had sent their first volleys into the opposing armies' ranks. Men had already fallen, and more fell as we watched, cut down by the iron arrowheads. I had to do something fast. People's lives were at stake, and one of those lives was my own father's.

"I have to stop this!" I said.

Although Grumble Belly circled above the battlefield, no one on the ground seemed to notice us. "I could fry them if you'd like," the dragon suggested, and his belly began to grumble.

"No," I said. "I don't want you to hurt them, either."

Eadric tapped my shoulder. "What kind of magic did the Green Witch use in the tapestry?" he asked. "Maybe you could do something like that."

"I don't know what she did. I'm going to have to come up with something on my own. Wait a minute." A bizarre picture had popped into my head. I couldn't keep from laughing, a deep-down belly laugh that made Grumble Belly snort blue flame and turn his head to look at me in surprise. It was loud, and I know I sounded strange, but it wasn't anything I could control. I had just had the most wonderful, impossible, amazing idea.

"What's so funny?" demanded Eadric when I'd started to calm down.

"You'll see," I said, wiping tears from my eyes. "Just

sit back and give me some room. First of all, I need a way to deliver a spell. Pointing my finger from up here wouldn't work very well. How about this?" I used my hands to shape a ball bigger than a witches' light. Although I hadn't asked it to be, the ball turned out to be green. "Now to add the right spell, and I think this one is perfect!"

Strangers came to steal our land,
To take what they could carry.
They're free to go, if they leave now,
As long as they don't tarry.

If they stay to fight a war,
They'll have to pay a price.
While they remain upon our land
They'll live as frogs or mice.

"You're turning an entire army into frogs or mice?" asked Eadric.

"Not the *whole* army," I said. "Just enough so they'll get the point. Grumble Belly, would you mind flying lower? Right over Beltran's army would be fine."

While the dragon swooped and turned, I tossed the ball as hard as I could, aiming for the center of the front line. The ball glittered as it fell, and some soldiers in the back shot arrows at it but missed. Grumble Belly flamed and turned the arrows to ash before they could hurt anyone.

When the ball hit the ground, it exploded in a shower of green droplets. The men closest to it disappeared immediately, then the men next in line disappeared as well. My father's men cheered as an ever-widening green circle devastated the front lines. It looked as though Beltran's men had simply vanished. It wasn't until the soldiers behind them pointed at the ground and began hopping around like they'd suddenly lost their minds that I knew that my spell had worked. Grumble Belly flew lower, and I saw that the ground was swarming with brown mice. Although the frogs blended in with the spreading green magic, I thought I saw a few of them as well.

"Good!" I said. "Now let's go see King Beltran."

"The king might listen to you better if you go armed," warned Eadric.

I nodded and hurried through the spell, making another green ball.

Grumble Belly flapped his wings, creating a wind that knocked over a half dozen foot soldiers. The archers raised their bows, but he ignored them and soared past the army before they could let any arrows fly.

The clanking of armor was loud when the knights turned to face us, but Grumble Belly began puffing smoke the moment he landed, and the knights seemed reluctant to engage an angry dragon. I could see only a little of the king's face beneath his helmet, since the metal came low over his brow and the nosepiece covered his nose. He was an old man with a short beard and thin lips, and his eyes were two dark smudges against a face turned pale. Jorge sat beside him, his long blond curls peeking out from under his helmet, his deep blue eyes watching me with disdain.

"King Beltran," I announced, "I am the Green Witch and protector of Greater Greensward. I demand that you leave our land at once."

The mounted knights muttered, their horses shifting restlessly, but the king raised his hand and the voices stilled.

"If you leave now," I said, "you may go home, but each man who stays to fight will turn into a frog or a mouse."

"What about the men you've already changed?" asked the king.

"Take them with you. They'll turn back into men once they cross the border into your kingdom."

"Don't believe her, Father," said Prince Jorge. "That's Emeralda, the princess you insisted I marry. I've seen the Green Witch, and she's older than that girl."

"Hello, Jorge," I said.

"'Your Highness' to you," he said, his nostrils flaring. "You were lucky that I was willing to marry you, but you were too stupid to know it. Is that the commoner who carried you off?"

"I'm not a commoner, and I didn't carry her off." Eadric sounded indignant. "I'm as much a prince as you are, Jorge, and I'll have you know that I'm going to marry Emma!"

Jorge took off his helmet. "Prince Eadric, is that you? I thought you looked familiar. Where did you get a dragon? I don't suppose you'd sell it? I'd look marvelous on a beast like that."

Grumble Belly's stomach rumbled, and smoke trickled out his nostrils. "Dragons aren't for sale!" I said as his muscles tensed under me.

"Then we have nothing more to talk about," Jorge said, setting his helmet back on his head.

"You can still marry him, girl," said King Beltran. "If your father gives me enough land, I'd be willing to ignore your foolishness."

"I didn't want to marry your son before, and I certainly don't want to marry him now. You'd better leave and never come back. I'm watching over this kingdom, and you aren't welcome here!"

"I see," said the king. "Then you leave me no choice but to use force to change your mind." Turning to the knights behind him, Beltran raised his hand and nodded. Without bothering to look at us again, the king and his son trotted toward the forest. Once the king was out of the way, his knights lifted their swords and urged their horses forward.

"I wish I'd brought Ferdy, but I didn't think I needed him when we went to the swamp," said Eadric.

"That's all right. I'm the one who's armed this time. These people don't seem to believe in magic unless it happens to them. I guess I'll have to give them a taste. Grumble Belly, I think it would have a greater impact from the air."

Snorting again, the dragon pumped his wings, and we rose above their heads, making the horses rear. A few of the knights slid off their horses' backs to the ground, where they lay struggling under their armor's weight. We hadn't gone far when archers began to shoot at us, so I didn't hesitate before throwing the next ball. It landed in the midst of the knights, and I was pleased to see that it didn't affect the horses, although their riders disappeared into the depths of their armor.

King Beltran and Prince Jorge had already moved out of my weapon's range and were fleeing the field when Grumble Belly flew after them. "And what about you?" I called while shaping another green ball with my hands.

"We'll go!" shouted the king. "Just leave us alone and let us gather our men!"

"Very well," I said. "You have one hour to collect your soldiers." Resting the ball between Grumble Belly's spikes, I leaned back against Eadric while the dragon's enormous wings carried us higher.

"Should I take you home now?" asked Grumble Belly, swerving over the remaining soldiers.

"Not yet, if you don't mind. I think we'd better stay and make sure they really do leave. I need to talk to my father, too. I'm sure he'd like to know what's happened."

We were higher than the treetops when Eadric and I leaned over to watch the soldiers scurrying about, collecting frogs and mice in their helmets and on their shields.

"I wonder how many will actually make it home," said Eadric.

I shrugged. "I don't know, but life as a frog isn't too bad." Squirming in my seat, I turned to face him. "I'm sorry if I seem to take you for granted sometimes. I dragged you into some awful predicaments, but you've helped me more than I could have dreamed possible. I appreciate everything you've done."

"Enough to give me a kiss?"

"Mmm," I said. The kiss was long and loving and I enjoyed every second of it.

After a time, Eadric pulled away to murmur, "You're wrong about one thing. Those were adventures, not predicaments. I like adventures, and maybe that's one of the reasons I'm crazy about you. When you're around, I never know what's going to happen next!"